D1600633

BEYOND THE DESERT

BEYOND
THE DESERT

40

BY
EUGENE MANLOVE RHODES

Introduction by
W. H. Hutchinson

UNIVERSITY OF NEBRASKA PRESS · LINCOLN

First Bison Book printing October, 1967

Con Razón

Eugene Manlove Rhodes was overlooked consistently, mayhap deliberately, by the self-anointed literary tastemakers of his time. He has been ignored by their successors since his death in that same year which saw *Beyond the Desert* appear in book form. *Imprimis*, he was a teller of tales, even as Robert Louis Stevenson, which was bad enough. Much worse was the fact that he told tales about the American West. The literati lumped his offerings with the mass of formula-fiction "westerns" they dismissed as a lamentable error of popular taste. For an added bar sinister, he wrote for the *Saturday Evening Post* which every right-minded *littérateur* knew was damned beyond redemption by middle-class mores. Finally, he was guilty in the 1930's of speaking out against what he described as the "Conrad Aiken-void" in American letters. Yet Rhodes has lived by virtue of a sub-culture "as select and discriminating as any that ever boosted a tenth-rate English poet into a first-rate reputation."

Bernard DeVoto also dubbed him "the novelist of the cattle kingdom," and went on record that Rhodes had produced the only fiction of that brief and violent segment of the American experience which transcended the fatuous solemnity of horse opera. Conrad Richter compared him to Joseph Conrad, another tale-teller, which is not minor praise, and J. Frank Dobie in a letter to this writer said: "A liberated mind, civilized perspective, and charm set him apart from all other writers on cowboy life. Rhodes had a better and more active mind than Wister, who became increasingly stuff-shirted with age." Then Walter Prescott Webb, who will do to take along as a historian of the American West, used the *Saturday Review* (Sept. 15, 1956) to limn the pioneer-as-artist.

He was tempered hard enough to be admired but a little too hard to be imitated. Hence men made legends of him while he lived. He once said that life is a disease and that the only cure for it is death. He was impudent towards life and impudent towards death. He hated more passionately than he did a felon the literary school of filth, and he deplored the [*literary*] group which taught youth that the main end of man is the middle.

And he believed above all else that the earth is a good place in which to spend a lifetime. . . . To write as 'Gene wrote one would have to live as 'Gene lived, and I know of no writer in this country, at Breadloaf or elsewhere, that has the guts to do that even if there was left a place to live that way.

Item 169 in a December, 1966, catalog issued by one of the most respected bookmen in and of the West bears witness to the continuing passion of the true Rhodesians: *Wrapping paper used to send a book with return signature of Rhodes $10.00.*

Rhodes barely had breached his teens when he arrived in Engle, New Mexico, "the year that Billy-the-Kid was killed." The frontier ended officially by Census Bureau pronouncement nine years later, and Frederick Jackson Turner gave it historical interment three years thereafter. Neither Bureau nor historian advised New Mexico or 'Gene Rhodes of its death and burial. Neither would have been believed if they had done so. The last American West remained pungently alive for all of Rhodes years in his chosen parish, and it was a noble one by any frontier measurement.

Bounded on the east by the Mescalero Apache Reservation in the high mountain country where *Beyond the Desert* has its setting, it reached westwards across the restless dunes of the White Sands, across purple ranges sheer and vast, to the slaunchandicular country beneath the Mogollon Rim. Its true Babylon was El Paso on the south, whence it angled northwestwards across the black-grama grasslands of the *Jornado del Muerto* to Socorro, and on beyond into the wind-washed, sun-warped, red-rock homeland of the Navaho.

He was in and of this land for twenty-five rounded years, and he lived each and all like a colt that keeps fishing for the bits. When in time he came to write about his parish and its people and, above all, their values, he preserved them in the clear amber of a joyous dancing illuminated prose. Upon what he wrote you may depend, as upon the shards and points and tree-ring datings of a vanished people.

What the railroad meant in the last westering surge of a restless breed was a part of his own life. Just so the plot of *Beyond the Desert* comes directly from the supreme need of the El Paso & North Eastern to find pure boiler water as it built across the alkali flats of the Tularosa Basin.

Long before manual labor for a daily wage involved him in this quest, he had learned the high cost of water for man and beast in the lands beyond the Hundredth Meridian. "Bay Ben had a reaching foot," he wrote, and in his land and in his time, the horses by which men lived and sometimes died were far beyond the play world of today's horse cultists.

His life knew violence for he lived it in a land of hazard, including the omnipresent hazard of the unknown that so erodes man's will today. Mine tunnel or stope could cave in without warning. The badger den unseen by man or mount could bring joint disaster in midstride. A pack rat about his nocturnal occasions could jolt a sleeping herd into stampede. The wrong word at the right time could trigger homicidal reflexes. "I have seen thirteen men killed," wrote Rhodes in later years. Unstructured chance, what some men woo as "Luck" while denying its existence, was accepted by Rhodes in life as he reflected it in his writings—without cavil or whine or preening.

His land and his life held outlaws—Black Jack Ketchum and Bill Doolin were his house guests —and his land and his life held very, very many who were not out of the same stock whence came 'Gene Rhodes. He learned from Ketchum and Doolin, from "Cherokee Bill" and Francisco Bojórquez and others, that there was no caste of lawfulness or pigment. It was how a man did what he did between a rock and a hard place that gave him stature among men, that made the basis for his judgment by his peers and this on their own terms.

Had he been asked to choose, Rhodes would have preferred Sisyphus to Sartre because he felt the tragic bond of the continuity of the generations and because he would have rejected, although the ailment was not in his lexicon of life, the narcissistic absurdity of nihilism. Yet was he an existentialist in the true and proper rooting of that abused word, because he stood out from, a self-styled "Ragged Individualist," a frontier society beset by rampant individuals. His code required him to act as he had to act, and to abide the consequences, without calling upon God, the government, or a sacred cause to attest the purity of his intentions. "I pay for what I break," he wrote, and his pinnacle of man's estate was "Master of no man and Servant of none."

As prickly with independence as a porcupine, he nonetheless knew his land's impositions for survival. So you will find the *group* in his stories but never will you find *groupthink*. Voluntary association made his groups coalesce because individual survival or true justice temporarily demanded it. It came about, too, as a condition of such employment as Rhodes, and others since, have called "working for the brand." Rhodes' romanticism, "Sir Walter Scott almost ruined me," sometimes overlaid reality. When it did, his version of group activity bore a striking resemblance to the antics of Athos and his friends. Even in these cases, lamentable though they may seem, each member of a Rhodesian group has sufficient iron in his bowels to remain his own whole man without submerging another to retain his wholeness.

Next to the infrequent and infrangibly virginal females in his stories, his weakest characterizations are those who wear the black hats of villainy. Even so they reflect his vision of his land's worst enemies. By and large, they do not work with their hands. Of deeper dye are those who betray their own code, whether it be Rhodes' code is of small import beside the act of betrayal, or who betray another's trust that they had accepted of their own volition. His bloated, swollen, Dickensian scoundrels are hall-marked by an appalling greed. "I learned deduction," he wrote, "from watching lawyers settling estates." So he used his paramount villains, as Balzac used misers and Faulkner the Snopeses, to decry the corrosion of cherished values by the acid of cupidity.

He used his heroes to hymn his conditioning by the frontier experience. More than twenty years of harvesting in the Rhodesian vineyard has not revealed one callow youth among them. Most of his heroes are between mid-morning and mid-afternoon of life, the fullest yet cruelest segment of man's span. Some of his heroes are past their sunset but are no more aware of it than are those who read about them. For twenty-five years he had known no such things as an end to freedom of individual action, or of mobility, or of limitless horizons, or of infinite chances to pick oneself from off the floor of life and try again. These were the four freedoms of life as he had lived it when he and his world were young and his circles had no centers.

Acutely personal reasons, including a warrant or so for his apprehension, caused Rhodes to remove himself from New Mexico in 1906. He was returned to the chipped-pottery crest of the San Andrés Range, the *querencia* of the bright mornings of his good years, in 1934. Suffering the claustrophobia of exile down all the years between, trembling Pegasus broke to a plow collar as it were, Rhodes fanned the memory-embers of his youth into prose.

In so doing he kept alive the forthright confidence, the joyous optimism, the you-be-damned integrity that three centuries of free movement into westward space once made his country's major and his own particular heritage. In so doing, he made real the ideal values of this heritage. Because he did this good thing does the "locoed cowpuncher from Engle" deserve his proper place in the frieze about the literary Pantheon of our westering. And it should be noted carefully that it has not been said that he idealized the real.

W. H. HUTCHINSON

Chico State College,
Chico, California

BEYOND THE DESERT

BEYOND THE DESERT

. .

CHAPTER I

On a blazing afternoon in July, three men journeyed from afar toward La Huerta, from three points of the compass.

Shane McFarland rode south and south from Gallows Hill and Malhecho through a cloudless day. A blistering day on the desert, far below him and to his right; no worse than a warm and friendly day where he rode high athwart a mighty slope toward a mountain on a hill; Star Mountain, pine black above a golden pedestal. A pedestal like an inverted saucer for shape, a pedestal which needed a hundred long miles and fifty to make a circuit at the base of it.

At his left, abreast him and far behind him, a long and loitering star-point of Old Star stretched far into the north. A short star-point of Old Star plunged headlong to westward, dead before him, barring his way. The great triangle between the long rampart and the short one was Catorce — Fourteen — so named from the 14 cattle ranch of old time. This July was more than half a lifetime ago. It was a time of panic, it was a time of drought, it was 1893. Range cattle were nine dollars a head, eight dollars, seven dollars, with no takers.

Shane McFarland, Easy McFarland, had no eyes for the desert, the long wide ribbon of the Mal Pais lava flow, the craters and cones of Cienfuegos, or for Wheel Mountain and Prairie Mountain far beyond, on the western rim of the world. He rode with averted head; perhaps because Catorce, once loved Catorce, lay below him. The old 14 brand was gone. Fenced Catorce was now a lost province, where Bat Cremony's idiot sheep fed on the short curly grasses, deep-rooted, drought-resistant. He rode in a mile-wide lane between the long fence of the Catorce leases and the long star-point spur.

Without warning, against wish and will, Easy's eyes turned to see, far below, the long, low buildings and wooden windmills of the home ranch. He thought with a pang of

Leslie Ellis and her wide brown eyes. Far away, forgotten. Hers had been a luckless marriage. Easy rode soberly up the narrowing lane.

Bay Ben had a reaching foot. They had started at six: the last water had been on the final trickle of Malhecho Creek, where it sank for the last time. From there, the high country had curved eastward in a gray crescent, and this pathless way had been bow-string straight to the southern horn of the crescent, never within two hours of any water or ranch-house. Three o'clock, half-past two. Thirty-six miles: bay Ben was brisk and strong, corn-fed. Less brisk, now; the last ten miles had been a slow, steady climb. While Easy was a middle-sized man — smallish, perhaps — yet, after all, Ben was just that size of a horse. Taking one thing with another, Ben was making three miles now as against four in the morning hours.

Ben's full name was Abou Ben Adams, but that was just between themselves, Ben and his master. Easy was a glutton for the reading of all printed matter that came within grasp of his capable hands; to the lasting mystification and amusement of his associates, most of whom read not at all. True, every one of them could finish, letter perfect, any sudden quotation from the labels of such cans, bags, sacks, or other containers as, in that place and day, were used for standard brands of coffee, sugar, salt, flour, condensed milk, pears, peaches, and other such. But that was compulsory. Men reeled off those few kind words with readiness who could not read at all, but had learned them by ear. By the custom of the country, if you made a slip — not being a newcomer — you were spread-eagled over a bed-roll and every man in camp put the chaps to you — or, as Englished, smote you, once and heartily, with a pair of leather leggings. They were earnest and studious men: which proves or disproves many educational theories.

All this to explain why Ben enjoyed two names, public and private. As for Easy, he was not only of middle-size, but also of middle-age. Thirty-five, forty, thirty? Along in there. A sprightly mouth beneath a brown mustache, a mouth fit for laughter; but there were lines that were not laughter lines. A dark face, smooth enough, pleasant enough: but the blue eyes, surprising in a face so dark, were the eyes of a man who had crossed many Rubicons; and the strong, active body, still swift and capable, had no longer the unconscious grace of youth. Middle-age. A hard age. There are only two ages that are harder.

They came to a gate in the pasture fence, a dim wagon-road that came through that gate from the home ranch. Close above them the great star-point ridge barred the way; a hundred tip-tilt limestone ledges, the dip to the east, high scarp to the west. Here the old road fluttered uncertainly, selected, as guide, one ledge from the hundred eligibles, turned abruptly west and followed between ledge and ledge in twisting loops as ledge and ledge turned in and back at each water-worn gorge, and so came breathless to the crest of the ridge: turned east again to follow that backbone ridge.

At that turning-point, the travelers made a halt, Ben for a much-needed rest and breathing in the shade of a powder-puff cedar; Easy to sit on a parapet cliff and to look down on the walled valley of Dorayme, south of this walling ridge and fifteen hundred feet below.

Here had been a pleasant settlement once, four and twenty little homes strung for six curly miles along the narrow valley of the tiny river; four and twenty brands of cattle to roam the grasslands, scarce fifty head in the largest brand; four and twenty little orchards and gardens: a little Catholic church, a little store, a little post-office on Saturdays — on which day a rider brought the mail from La Huerta, far south beyond the next star-point ridge of Star Mountain. The odd name had been given because there had been hardly a child of all the children of all those four and twenty homes who could not work magic with fiddle, guitar, or accordion — mouth-harp at the worst of it — as naturally and unconsciously as they rode their small, swift ponies. Not from

study: that simple music was part of un-
hurried life, like breathing or sleeping. Valley, river, and settlement took name from the
musical scale. Do, re, mi. There had been
dances on Saturdays as well as mail. Saturday
nights. A place of mirth and laughter — then.

Not now. A money-making place, now.
Jake Fowler had bought out the four and
twenty homes, at a fair price for some, at
foreclosure prices for many. Families were
scattered and forgotten, store and church
closed, the little orchards were dying, neglected. All the water of Dorayme Creek
was used in the upper valley, where the flow
was greatest, to irrigate one crop — alfalfa.
Jake Fowler managed to get irrigation
acreage to double that used by the wasteful,
laughing Dorayme people. The alfalfa was
tended by hired hands, brown bachelors;
stacked in the fields where it was grown. The
wide grasslands were leased and stoutly
fenced. Jake bought yearling steers and
matured them under fence, feeding from the
vast alfalfa stacks at need, holding them over
another year if prices were bad, holding

prime beef always ready for Government contracts at Indian Reservations or Army Posts, always sure of contracts, with better beef than could be had from the open range. The prudent man grew great.

'Ill fares the land,' said Easy McFarland — as naturally as the children of lost Dorayme had plucked a guitar. He supplemented the quotation with bitter words of his own. Shane McFarland had Cassandra's gift, and her penalty: to foresee truly, and not to be believed.

He swung into the saddle and turned up the ridge with the old road. A narrow road, a steep road, a dangerous road, dodging to left and right of spiny knobs on this backbone ridge: a little-used and neglected road, ugly with little gullies and heaps of rubble. Old Tom Copeland had built it for himself. No one else lived on this Jack-and-the-beanstalk road. Tom, thrifty soul, had brought in supplies from Las Vegas, by way of Gallows Hill: sugar by the sack, coffee by the case, cut prices. Tom was dead now, and careless Bud packed in from near-by La

Huerta — small packs, poor man's prices; one tenth as far as Las Vegas and ten times as many trips: a losing traffic.

In a last desperate scramble, ridge and road merged with the main mass of Star Mountain: a rolling country, a red country of oaks and junipers and the beginnings of pine lands, with red sugarloaf hills to his left and above, and a box canyon gashed through limestone to his right, narrow and dark, looping in a long double curve: falling in one appalling drop of two thousand feet into unimaginable darkness where no sun ever shines; Black Gorge, a freak of the Fire Gods in their mountain-making.

Rest River falls roaring into Black Gorge, and the unceasing complaint of tangled echoes struggles up from the deeps to trouble the land. In flood time, all the valley throbs with witch-drumming. Three miles as the crow flies, twice that by the tortured channel; and at the lower end of that box canyon, there is no Rest River. Somewhere in that untrodden blackness the little river goes underground: to reappear as the Dorayme

Creek, a mile and more down the valley. With diminished volume; somewhere in that dark and dreadful journey, half of Rest River is forever lost. Rest River was a joke, at its best. Flood water of great rains aside, Rest River was an easy jump at its widest. But you could step across Dorayme.

The air was fresh and cool, spicy with the scent of greenwood near, an unimaginable delight after the low country. And at the next curve a gateway opened in the hills to show an unguessed country: a hidden valley walled with low spiky granite or piled porphyry, masked on three sides by higher hills of limestone, heavily timbered, and with the great peak of Star Mountain, vast, ominous, and steep, splintered porphyry, looming above all the south, late lingering snow on all the northern slopes and deep drifts in the gashed ravines, the bald crest above the timber-line. The basin was roughly oval, with some five or seven miles for its greatest diameter, thickly studded with bold knobs and knolls of granite, among which Rest River wound its tortuous way, bordered by a heavy growth of oaks, maples, black locusts, and walnut.

All the narrow branching meadows were red and white with grazing cattle. This hidden valley was known as El Olvidado, The Forgotten — a name which the Mexicans shortened to Olvidado, and pronounced Olvidow. But Old Tom Copeland always called it High Dudgeon. The Mexican name was the apt one. This was the world's end.

A rail fence, new and unweathered, crossed the gap from cliff to cliff; a double log house nestled under towering locust trees; two large rooms with a covered passageway between them. A log barn peeped through a windbreak cluster of trees. Easy got down to open the bars. A bell-mouthed hound charged to meet him, baying ferociously; a thunderous voice called reproaches from the house. Easy drove the dog back, led bay Ben down to the houseyard gate, and left him there.

Bud Copeland sat in the passageway with his feet in a tub of water. Easy eyed him with mild surprise.

'Why, Bud, what in the world are you doing?'

'I thought I'd wash my feet and see if I could stay here.' Bud was a youngish man, thin of build and something knobby. Hollow cheeks accentuated the square angle of his jaw. His gray eyes were friendly eyes, the quirky mouth was a friendly mouth, for all that it was marred by one missing tooth above and one below. On his right hand, the little finger and the next had been cut off, together with half of the middle finger, and his nose was slightly awry; giving him, altogether, the appearance of a battered citizen. 'That hound, Easy, he's just noisy. Sounds like he was aiming to gnaw your shin bones, but he don't mean any harm. Just tell him "Down, Mose," and he shuts right up.'

'I spoke to him,' said Easy. 'That wasn't what I said, exactly, but I spoke to him.'

Bud reached for a towel. 'You lead your nag down to the barn, and I'll be startin' supper. Barley in the bin and good barley hay in the mow.'

CHAPTER II

BEARSKINS on the floor, antlers on the wall, a jolly backlog crackling in the fireplace: at this altitude, even July nights were chill. Dishes were washed, high-heeled boots discarded for soft moccasins: Bud and Easy, feet high, sprawled back in vast rustic rocking-chairs wrought from hickory by the patient labor of Old Tom, becarved, braided, twisted, shaped and scraped and varnished. Settle, beds, gunrack, table, kept the mellow memory of him. So humble a thing as a bootjack was not sawed and angular, but curved and carved by loving artistry of those dead hands; massy door-frames, window-frames, adze-hewn, all but spoke his name.

A steaming kettle swung from a crane in the fireplace: a small bottle and small glasses stood on a small table, together with a glass tobacco jar, a nickled lamp. The small table was within easy reach of the two chairs; pipes were going.

'Son,' said Easy, 'how long since our last get-together? Do you remember?'

'Let me see. Fall round-up was a year ago. Golly, it's been nigh on to eighteen months. Fine neighbors we are — and us livin' barely a hop, skip, and jump away from each other. Only, of course, you trade north while I go to La Huerta.'

Easy examined the beamed ceiling with curious eyes. 'At that time, if I remember rightly, you were some down at the mouth, weren't you?'

Bud laughed cheerfully. 'Sure thing. Worrying about my mortgage. Cattle was down to eighteen dollars.'

'Yes, yes. And now they are eight. This being thus, we come by natural and easy stages to why and wherefore I drifted down to see. I come to name a little dicker to you — so you could be thinking it over. Not to be prying into your private affairs, but just because it will be lot and part of our trade, if any, how about your mortgage? You never told me how-come. I supposed you was well fixed.'

'I was — if I had any sense. After Dad died, I fooled away one year's steer money takin' a look around. New York, Washington, and the elephants. Then a winter in California. Seein' the world. Then two or three years lookin' into booze and poker —— Aw, you know all this.'

'I heard a rumor, or perhaps two. Nothing definite. Nobody seemed to think it was any of their business, or to be very much surprised. Or shocked. Or indignant.'

'Well, that's the way it was. So I took a tumble to myself. About that time, I got a chance to buy another little brand. About two hundred head. Nice stuff. Cattle was about twenty-eight or twenty-nine dollars, and I could buy these for twenty-five, quick trade, cash money. So I up and mortgaged my ranch and the Sliding H brand to Jake Fowler — including the bunch I bought. Five thousand, five years to pay it. Nearly a lifetime. That was week before last, seems like. Five years is up come November. Just after steer harvest.'

Easy nodded. 'And you've been getting less and less for your steers, every year. Twenty dollars, fifteen, ten. We thought in '88 that the big prices would go on forever. I did, myself.'

'That ain't all, Easy. I've got the best summer range in the territory — but it is all cold and snow in the winter. So, Catorce and Dorayme cattle used to come up here in the summer. Then, when snow came, the Sliding H cows, every one, went down in Catorce and Dorayme, to winter. Fair enough. Handy as a pocket in a shirt. Well, you know what happened. Jake Fowler bought out Dorayme and fenced. Bat Cremony bought out the Catorce and fenced. All the winter range I've got is from here down — the Red Beds, and it's pretty cold even there at times. Plus the little narrow strips between the fences and the hills, too far from water. I'm fencing across the gaps to save all the grass in the Red Beds for winter. Of course, some of the cows get out over the roughs, but I keep most of them up here all summer. But I didn't begin fencing soon enough. My stuff isn't doing well. Small calf crop. I had nearly as many cattle three years ago as I have now, and they was worth three times as much.'

'Aren't you forgetting something, Bud?'

'What?'

'Good old ten per cent. Tell you what — all the wars, cyclones, floods, fires, earthquakes, and shipwrecks haven't caused as much misery, all told, as six per cent. I say this on the best authority: I guessed it out myself. That is six per cent, but ten per cent is blue ruin. Go on. Your story interests me strangely.'

'This story is about done. I've got six hundred to six-fifty head of cows and a foolish little bunch of mares that don't pay and that I keep just because Dad liked 'em and took so much pleasure in them. If I sell each and every head, there won't be enough to pay the mortgage. So I'll have a ranch without any cattle — unless Jake will renew.'

'Why, you long, loose-jointed, trifling, worthless, horse-stealing, whiskey-drinking, poker-playin', ignorant, no-account ——'

'You needn't speak kindly to me,' said Bud. 'I ain't sick.'

'Don't you know that Jake Fowler isn't going to renew your mortgage?'

'Oh, he might. Cattle prices will come up, soon or late. They must.'

'You miserable, warty, horned toad — that's why he won't renew. He gets your cattle cheap and holds them till he doubles his money and then some. And he'll cling tight to your ranch, just for a keepsake.'

'Shucks, I won't lose the ranch. I can all but pay out, and I can get me another bunch of cattle on shares, maybe. This is a good ranch.'

'Sure it is. That's why Jake Fowler wants it. Good summer range. He will fence it tight, high and strong, and keep Dorayme for winter. You'll be short a thousand on your mortgage, and five hundred on interest. Nobody will lend money on cattle now, the way things are. Jake will bid you in for face of the mortgage, lock, stock and barrel, and not one bid against him. There's your fortune told.'

'Do you think so?'

'Think so? I know it. That is the way

swollen fortunes get swelled up. So here is where I come in. If you are in the proper frame of mind — and to get you in the proper frame of mind was exactly why I broke out into prophecy — you just listen to me.

'I've got about eight hundred head. And a pretty fair desert range. Well and good. But there is more than plenty cow-stealing close to me and coming closer. What I see is a range war, three years away, and maybe sooner. I'm not crowded yet — but I have no protection. Anyone can dig a well and get bad water and overstock the range. They'll do that, soon or late. If this railroad ever comes, that we hear so much about, it will be soon. Long-legged Texans drifting by to look see. That's the lay.

'Well and good. Old Man Kinney, he wants my ranch. Offers me ten dollars a head if I throw in my wells and water-holes. Eight thousand — and I held out for twenty a little over three years ago. There you are. If I stay, I'll have to kill or be killed. Old Clay Kinney don't mind that, but I do. I'm a wise old bird, I am. You bear that in

mind. Study it over. If you say the word,
I'll sell, pay off your mortgage, and salt
away the balance on joint account, for half
your ranch and brand. And I'll bring my
own saddle horses. Won't sell them to
Kinney. He's death on horses.'

'That's a mighty liberal offer, Easy.'

'It isn't stingy, no. Still, you bear it in
mind that I've been drinking alkali water
for seven years. You've got soft water here
— the only good water in all the country
you can see in four looks. You take a long
think. Not a stingy offer, but I'm not
cheating myself. I'm due to lose if I stay
where I am. That range won't stand over-
stocking. Besides — cattle will be up. We'll
be fixed to hold over our steer crop to two-
year-olds — three if necessary — and make
big money doing it. Two of us. We'll raise
all the barley hay in the world and feed it in
the cold spells. Why not? Or get us a well
of bad water out on the desert, close to here
as we can get it, and move our stuff down
every winter — two of us and no wages to
pay. That isn't all either. I hate Jake

Fowler's lights, lungs, liver, and gizzard. The spoil of the poor is in his house. Somebody ought to cut him off at the pockets, and I'd like to be the one. For another thing, I like Olvidado. Always did. It's like heaven after that blistering desert.'

'It is only fair to tell you,' said Bud, 'there are drawbacks to Olvidado. Year before last, I overslept one morning, and missed the summer completely.'

They rode together through the mazes of Olvidado the next day, planning joyously. They would build a tank, or try a well, outside Catorce fence, to utilize that narrow strip of lowland for winter range. They would build a broad trail down to Dorayme, and use the grass in the hills, outside of the Fowler fence, for winter range, they could be sure of shallow water at the mouth of Black Gorge. They would ship out the mares, that nipped the grass too close, and were a losing venture at best. They rode in the rough country to inspect Bud's stop-gap fences there, built to keep the Sliding H cows from climbing east across the divide into John Marble's country; they found, in a high glade, a small dozen from Marble's wild bunch that had gone around the fences. The dozen did a dash for the brush. Bud was at their heels, rope down, building a loop, but the cows crashed into thick timber before Bud could make his throw. Shane came then, while Bud was doing up his rope.

'That clearing was too short at one end,' said Bud. 'See that line-back ONO cow with the yearling?'

'Listen, fellow, I'm no brush-popper. I live out in the open plain, and we don't have to explode when we work our cattle. We saunter after them, and if we waste one loop, we ejaculate about it a spell, and then try again. Line-back cow? Yearlin'? I saw a red-and-white streak — cows or something. I looked around to speak to you about it, and you wasn't there. Just me, all alone. Is that hospitable? I ask you.'

'Me and John Marble tried twice for that yearling of his, over on his side of the hill, and this is my second try over here. That bunch is sure snaky. Guess John will have to shoot 'em for beef. They won't leave the woods. No use to brand 'em if you never see them again. Eat 'em, says I; that's what I do with mine when they try to go wild on me.'

They rode slowly, zigzag, through mountain meadows blue with asters, and circled the walling hills. They noted the limit of the patented land along Rest River; Tom Copeland's homestead and pre-emption, Bud's homestead, four hundred and eighty acres in all, strung out long and narrow, to cover three devious miles of Rest River; planned that Easy should homestead another hundred and sixty acres; so turned happily homeward in the late afternoon.

'Mind you, Bud,' said the older man. 'I may be wrong about Jake Fowler. Maybe he only wants his ten per cent. Just barely possible, especially since he has never gone in for raising cattle — only for marketing cattle that someone else has raised. He may not want your stuff. If he will let you renew, by any chance — you stick it out. In two or three years prices will be up so you can sell half your cattle and pay him off. That would beat going snooks with me — if he'll let you renew. This ranch is worth more than your cattle. Some day if the railroad comes, and the rich folks find out about this place, they're going to pay big money to come up here in the summer. I judge that this is just about the finest place in the whole round world, for looks.'

'In the summer time, yes,' said Bud. 'Fishing, too. Never have to use any bait, even. Just promise 'em a grasshopper, and out they come.'

'You sidle on down to La Huerta tomorrow and put it up to Jake. Promise him a grasshopper. Make him see that if he forecloses, cattle will be down to nothing and he'll lose money, and that if he renews, it will be perfectly safe, because cattle are sure to come up. Maybe he'll bite. Listen, Bud. The old New Mexico storekeepers are the finest ever, our best citizens and our best loved men. They look out for everyone, and do a good turn for someone every time they get a chance, and make their own chances. But this lousy Jake Fowler makes his profit from hard bargains with misery and misfortune. The strong thief and the sneak thief wish their victims to be prosperous — but this louse dreams of dealing with despair. He stabbed me in the field by Tewkesbury.'

CHAPTER III

ON THAT same afternoon through which Shane McFarland rode past Catorce, two other men, from two other compass points, fared wearily through the glaring heat, from the west, from the southwest, heading for La Huerta.

Mr. Anson Hunter came from the southwest, the one passenger in La Huerta stage, which made two trips a week from Cibola and civilization to La Huerta. Cibola was the county seat.

That stage was no coach, but a sagging and rattling buckboard, with the mailsacks and the passenger's bag, tarpaulined together, lashed and double lashed behind the one seat. That seat was unsheltered from sun or rain — upon which fact the passenger made acid comment. The driver spread his empty whip hand, palm up, to deny responsibility.

'You might name it to Jake Fowler,' he said. 'He's got the contract. I'm nothing but a tobacco-chewin' hirelin'. Still and but,

I know this much, the big idea is to carry the mail; the comfort of passengers not bein' considered. You might almost say that there ain't any passengers. Them Cienfuegos citizens they got plenty hawses, all the time there is, and no money a-tall.'

A natty and pleasing passenger when he stepped into the buckboard at Cibola; a wilted, wrinkled, dusty, sweat-stained passenger when he stepped out at Westgate, after four hours of red sand and climbing ridges. Westgate was not a town, but a wide low pass between two twisting mountain ranges: Infeliz and Derredor. The stage station was well east of the divide, at the first spring in the pass. There had been no house and no water between Cibola and Westgate. There would be one house and one well in the next seventy miles, obliquely across the desert; Guffy's Well, stage station, halfway from Westgate to La Huerta. The 'stage' stopped at Westgate for another team, another driver, and a frugal supper. The mail, like others, preferred to cross the desert by night.

The traveler might well have turned his eyes down toward Cienfuegos, the Valley of a Hundred Fires, or glanced across that seabroad plain to where the low sun blazed on the cliffs of the Djinns and the Golden Cape.

He did neither. That traveler had once spent the best part of a year in Cienfuegos, loathing every hour of every day and every yard of every mile, as a silky-satiny soul loathes denim and jeans. He washed up in the tin basin with a bar of yellow soap and as he dried his fine hands on the coarsest of all fresh towels, his strong chin went up and his bold nose came down, twitching to a crooked sneer, while a full red lip curled up to a cruel snarl. 'Someone will pay for this!' said Anson Hunter.

Down grade, sidling roads, freshness of twilight winds, big stars near and bright, the smooth level of the plain, comfort from the cool canteen, good wheeling, brisk hoofs in a soothing rhythm, drowsiness, lurching sleep: then ridges, chuck holes, powdered chalk, something amiss, sensed in his jolting and uneasy slumbers; smarting eyes, and aching back — Guffy's Well. Coffee and cold beef by a flaring lamp — black coffee that was salty and bitter, made from water from a brackish well that was still the best water from foothill to foothill. Fresh horses and a third driver. The road followed the sluggish contours of a vast lava flow, or cut across from cape to cape of deep bays; a slow drag of sand, snatches of sleep and evil dreams, half-waking to discomfort of aching back, aching neck, aching sides. Brisk going again, stars burning close and low, scratching of bushes on the spokes, grinding of wheels in gravel — a glint of day.

Hunter roused up in the half-light, groaning, straightened his weary back, moistened a handkerchief from the canteen and dabbed at his dust-burned eyes.

'Get a good sleep?' said the driver.

Anson Hunter growled. A thin chill was in the air. He buttoned his coat tightly and humped his back.

'Take this blanket we're settin' on and wrap hit around you, if you're cold,' said the driver. 'Hit'll get right nippy 'tween now and sun up.'

Hunter took the blanket, with, after a space, a grudged and mumbled word of thanks. Dim daylight grew clear. The desert lay below them. They were climbing the first slopes of the long low ridges that fell away to the plain from the base of Star Mountain.

'Soon be there now,' said the driver. 'Only ten short miles from La Huerta down here. But it is fifteen long miles from here to there, going up. Steep? Oh, man!'

Hunter looked back once. The great lava flow was black and bleak below him, and the three low craters where that lava had bubbled up from central fires. To right and left, close or far, were scattered buttes and cones, each with its own blot of lava, great or small — most of it overblown with sand. Cienfuegos was a *bolson* country — a basin with no drainage outlet. Little streams from the higher mountains, flood waters in storm — if they ever reached the sea it was by some underground channel.

In the west the cliff-face of Los Nuevos was moon white, notched against the sky. He turned his face back to Star Mountain. A most irregular star, with snaky prongs more like the arms of a devilfish than star-points, an eight-pointed star, crest and higher ridges black with pine. Of all the many ranges about Cienfuegos, only Star Mountain and Los Genios, the Djinns, were high enough for pine.

The largest star-point wandered away to the south and southeast to merge uncertainly with the Djinns. A short, straight, steep star-point plunged westerly to the desert. In the angle so made, La Huerta perched, high above the desert heat and below the cold of the mountain mass. Borachón 'River,' Drunkard River, swift and small, had been turned from its channel and led southward to the first narrow curving shelf below the mountain proper, to water La Huerta, The Garden; a green and terraced town, a curving town, a long and narrow town, with fingers and thumb of orchard and farmlet on the smoother ridges as they fell away from the narrow shelf.

Woodsmoke of early chimneys rose from the darkness before them. Behind, below, the desert was ablaze with light, but the shadows were deep about them still as they toiled up a winding road. They came to good grass, shortish; to red and white of cattle, to bands of horses, to pools of water in the old channel of the Borachón fed by waste water from the farmlands above; to green cottonwoods kept alive by that waste. The sun came up for them while shadows were still dark over La Huerta; the sun was an hour high in La Huerta itself when they reached the first tinkling *acequía* and turned down the winding street. Green cottonwoods arched above them, windows and doors were open, families breakfasted *al fresco*, cows were being milked at pasture gates, fowls strutted and clucked and chattered in orchards. They passed by school and church, saloon and store, and so came to the Garden House, a low hostelry, four square under great trees.

Breakfast and bath — with a sneer for the one bathroom of the Garden House. Hunter was for bed. Wearily he went to his room. As he drew the curtain, he paused momentarily to look out on the long, dark, deep-shaded street, and children scampering to school. Again the bold nose came down and twisted to a sneer, again the corner of a red lip curled in scorn, and Anson Hunter said again,

'*Someone will pay for this.*'

CHAPTER IV

SAM CLARK reached the summit of Los Nuevos about three in the afternoon. The crest of Los Nuevos, New Mountain, is also the eastern edge. Los Nuevos has been tilted up like a hinged trapdoor, violently and all at once. The east side is a succession of cliffs, and all drainage is to the west. Sam sat on the highest rimrock and smoked. All Cienfuegos was plain to be seen. Half a hundred dead craters, ant-hill cones or ant-hill pyramids. Two lava beds, the great oval splotch to the south, the greater Mal Pais to the north, a river of stone; what had been a river of seething lava, seeking a level as water does, following the valley of an ancient water-course, creeping crookedly and cater-cornered across the great plain, spreading there in the low places, narrowing here between twisting hills, spreading again and cooling as it came to all the weird shapes of spilled ink on blotting-paper. A mile wide, five miles wide, fifteen miles at the widest, near the south end of it.

Midway of the widest place, the molten stream had split, turned right and left by higher ground, joining again, leaving a great round island of the old plain, white and startling in the black lava. This island was not to be seen from the desert, for the fire-river had cooled in dreadful bubbles, high above the plain, ten feet high, twenty, thirty. The island was visible only from the summit of Los Nuevos or from the upper slopes of Star Mountain. Rumor said there was water there, bad water, but drinkable, and a secret trail, twisting between broken bubbles; and that this island had been a hiding-place, last refuge of the hunted. Few believed this. But Sam knew it: knew the trail, and the name of that refuge. Fiddler's Green, 'fifteen miles beyond hell.' His eyes narrowed, and he spat over the cliff in re-membrance. Fiddler's Green was the metro-polis of rattlesnakes.

Sam's horse was a buckskin, big but thin and drawn. He stood droop-hipped and weary from the long climb. Sam spoke to him now. 'Thix thouthand feet up and no way down. Come on, Buck. We gotta get acroth Thienfuegoth.' Sam Clark was known as 'Lithpin Tham.'

But there was a way down, and Lithpin Tham knew it: a knowledge shared by less than a dozen men; an outlaw trail. For a young man, it was surprising how many things Lithpin Tham knew — all of them reprehensible. How to slip a cut, to deal seconds, to high-grade ore, to change a brand — things like that. The present journey, like most of Tham's journeys, was in search of some place where he was not unwelcome. He had outworn his welcome in Target, Tripoli, Salamanca, Hillsboro, Cibola, Socorro, Ridgepole, and twenty towns besides: shiftless at best, always a tinhorn gambler, often a petty crook. Not enterprising, hardly even a crook — a crook's helper, used and double-crossed and thrown aside. Like a chameleon, he took the color of his surroundings, and he companioned with the worst. Fanciful fellows, one or two, had been troubled, once or twice, with an uneasy guess that but for this ludicrous handicap of speech, better folk might have been kinder to Sam Clark, and that life as Sam Clark might have been different, and easier, than life as Lithpin Tham.

Star Mountain was due east, fifty miles away, fronting the wide opening between the big lava beds. North of Star Mountain, Gallows Hill was dim along the sky. That country was one of two places in Tham's world where he was not an outcast. The other place was a dim high valley where Tham had once played the man — under extreme provocation. Wise for once, Tham had decided not to go back to the people of that valley, judging that when they knew him better they would like him less. But his heart was warm to remember that somewhere men spoke of him kindly. That was not to be spoiled by going back.

Cienfuegos was different. At twenty, after an imbecile gun-fight at Alma, where both Tham and his antagonist were shot up, with neither much the worse for it, Tham had worked for the Rafter X, between Old Star and Gallows Hill. For two years he had been watermason, responsible for windmills, springs, pipelines, tanks. A little startled by his adventure at Alma, Tham had done fairly good work — the first year. Not so good, the second. Booze at Catorce, too many poker games. He had left by way of Fiddler's Green, in bad company. It was that or be killed. Tham knew too much. Still, no one knew of the Fiddler's Green episode. The Rafter X would think Tham had just drifted. The Rafter X had sold out now, and sheep had taken that country and Catorce — or so he had heard. Still, Tham hoped to get a job somewhere. Maybe he would do better, this time. *Likely!*

The way down from Los Nuevos was not a trail, but a remembered maze. The procedure was simple. Going down through one certain break of a hundred breaks in the upper rimrock, you turned to the left between ledges until you came to a gap in the lower ledge, went down that, then to the right to a certain gap in the next cliff below — not the first gap, or the second — then down, and to left or right, as the case might be to exactly the right break in the next ledge — and so on and on. There was no trail, no blaze, no monument. The way was overgrown with *ocotillo* and cactus and stunted bushes, blocked by rock slides, to be cleared away with pain. His last exploit at Yeltes had been particularly unsavory. Hence his choice of roads. Yeltes would have no notion which way he went. No one had seen him in two days of riding, mostly at night.

Tinhorn, weakling, crook, Lithpin Tham had one sure friend. The Buck horse followed cheerfully, on a loose rein, along that dizzy path. To Buck, Tham was the man of men, and his the one loved voice.

As the plumb-line falls, it was the better part of a mile down the cliffs. Buck and Tham made it in something over two hours. There was good grass on the lower slopes. It was a year of great drought, so the desert grasses would be worthless: Tham unsaddled and staked Buck to graze. There was a cumbrous canteen on the saddle, a slender store of food wrapped in his coat and tied behind the saddle. Tham shot a rabbit and broiled it on a stick. That made supper, with water from the canteen — sparingly — and a few crackers. Very few. Crackers made you thirsty.

'You fill up, old-timer, and I'll thleep a few. We'll go over to Magnethia Thprings in the cool, lay over in the heat, and get to La Huerta by early bedtime tomorrow.'

The Ellenyard rode high in the sky when Tham awoke. Tham's eye measured that height and then turned to the Big Dipper for comparison and confirmation. 'Half-path ten, maybe eleven. C'me on Buck, we gotta drag it.'

He gave a good rubbing to Buck's back, and shook the saddle blankets carefully before saddling. He took one small swallow from the canteen, and sighed. Magnesia Spring, midway of the desert, was vile drinking with only one good quality — that it was moist. Tham had a little more than a quart of good water to see him through fifty miles, and poor old Buck had only the bitter water of Magnesia.

Tham rode craftily, nursing a road-weary horse; the easiest of mincing trots where the footing was good, a walk of Buck's choosing in rotten ground. Buck's choosing was to push on right horsefully. Briskness was beyond what his legs could do, but he reached out sturdily. After a time they came to a dim trail, joined presently by other dim trails until it became a plain trail. Here the wild horses roamed, buying freedom at the price of all discomfort through all their days. Sam smoked, and talked to Buck, and sang interminable songs untunefully,

'O, ith curth your gold and your thilver too,
And curth the girl that don't prove true.'

Buck did not mind the lisp, or the high cracked voice. So the warm night wore on. Between daylight and sun up they sighted the low mound that marked Magnesia Spring, where Tham proposed to petrify until late in the afternoon.

It was not to be. There was a dead cow in Magnesia Spring — a very dead cow. Tham rode on for a hundred yards, and dismounted. Buck nosed inquiringly. What were they going to do now?

'Buck, I know one horth and one man that ith goin' to thee thorrow. We've got to puth on to water. But from now on I'll thpell you. I'll walk two or three mileth and then ride two or three mileth, even Thephen. Thith will be one bad day.'

He drank a swallow of warm water from the canteen, loosened the cinches, hung belt and six-shooter to the saddle-horn, scowled at his high-heeled boots, and led the way in the soft trail, straight into the rising sun.

CHAPTER V

LA HUERTA, The Garden, was a community of small farms. La Huertans were mostly Mexicans, but there was a liberal sprinkling of American blood. Lawyer, doctor, merchant, clerk; Father Giron, the jolly French priest: miller, blacksmith, saloon-keepers, gamblers, a preacher, a hotel-keeper, and school-teachers. The last were fixtures. Two of them were sedate mothers, and the principal was a sprightly grandmother. The school was La Huerta's boast and treasure.

Because of that school, small ranches in the mountains roundabout acquired each one a farmlet in La Huerta. Schooling, fruit, vegetables, eggs, milk, butter, shade and playfellows for the children, flowers and friends for the mothers; but schooling most of all. The men went back to the stony hills to work the cattle. La Huerta claimed as its own a story that was old when Greece was young. A father was going back to work after a long visit. His youngest shook hands with him. 'Papa,' said the urchin, 'can't you come and see us again, some-time?'

Every house had its little garden and vine-yard, a little orchard, apples, cherries, peaches, and nectarines; hens and ducks, milk cows, a shady pigpen; tiny fields of alfalfa, wheat and corn, thrifty patches of frijoles and chili. No Mexican so poor but he had a mare or two on the free range of the foothills, hardly a boy without a pony of his own; and most families had ten or a dozen cows. There was no big brand near-by: scat-tered cowmen ran small herds on the slopes below the town, or at springs in the lower hills; no crowding yet. The drive to market was too hard for this range to be desired by the covetous. No place is more cheerful than uncrowded cow country, and no place worse than a crowded one.

Since La Huerta had everything it needed, you will not be surprised to learn that the citizenry was discontented. La Huerta hun-gered and thirsted for a railroad, ardently desired that the new railroad, the Bee Line, long surveyed — surveyed thrice over, to be

exact — would build its twice accursed line
and be quick about it. To be sure, the railroad would not actually come to La Huerta.
Too high. Up in the eave-spouts. The road
would follow the plain, skirting the far-flung
slopes of Star Mountain; twelve miles away,
at the nearest line of survey stakes, twenty
miles at the farthest one. Fifteen miles was
nothing for people who waited for fall rains
to make it possible for the steer drive to
cross the desert to market, waited for fall
rains to do the year's freighting and the
year's visiting, and who stayed strictly at
home through summer and spring. Besides,
there would be a branch line to La Huerta,
in time, on its way to bring down lumber
from the summit. So La Huerta dreamed
and said.

Unexplainably, four years had gone by
since the first survey and the railroad had
not been built yet. But it would come. It
would be three hundred miles shorter than
any road from K. C. to the coast. It would
have to come. Lads of twenty, thirty, and
so on up to sixty, had gone on long journeys

with strings of small horses, returning after prolonged absence with smaller strings of larger horses. These larger horses had been broken to harness, with intensive education to plow and scraper work. Such training was of great benefit to the community ditch and to such fields as were imperfectly level — which fields were straightway smoothed and terraced for better irrigation. There would be fabulous wages for men and scraper teams when the railroad came, said La Huerta.

Half a dozen of these teams had found work already. Jake Fowler and Bat Cremony — the town's strong men, financially — had given closest consideration to the most probable site of all possible sites for the expected station on this hypothetical railroad. Down the straightest ridge north of the old river-bed, the strong men reasoned, the pipeline must come to bring Borachón water for refreshment of thirsty engines. This straight ridge gave the shortest route to the plain, free from danger of breakage by the brief, violent floods of the rainy season. And for average vantages of grade and distance, the central line of survey stakes was the likeliest to be followed at this place. Nothing venture, nothing gain — and these two were all for gaining. Accordingly, they took out papers for a tentative townsite, and now had a gang of men tentatively grubbing out mesquite bushes and lightly leveling to a small semblance of squares and streets.

A busy scene: plow and scraper, axes chopping on mesquite, teams yanking up mesquite roots with a stout chain and dragging them away. Camp was precisely where the water-tank must be, according to the two strong men, if the pipeline was to be the shortest line between two given points, and those points the north end of Borachón Dam and the nearest stake on the middle survey line. A regulation chuck-wagon was equipped with a wide awning, a double-sized tarpaulin stretched between wagon and two stout poles, tightly guyed to mesquites yet ungrubbed. The shade of that awning was the dining-hall — now occupied only by Bat Cremony himself, who with a bed-roll for a seat, was deep in his favorite book, an account book, casting up expenses of the joint venture. A star glittered on his broad breast, and a Colt's .45 hung from a broad belt. Bat was deputy sheriff, the only deputy east of the desert. That broad belt was also a long belt. It had to be. For if Bat's burly chest was broad and thick, the engirdled section was broader and thicker. Not fat exactly; the man was gross. Thighs, calves, and feet were heavy and thick, his arms were thick, his neck was thick, with thick jowls to make more square a big face, harsh and hard. Beyond the chuck-wagon stood Bat's 'hack,' a light spring wagon, with a square and sturdy top for cover from the sun. Harness and collars were draped at dashboard corners. Bat had just driven down from town.

At a judicious distance to leeward — which was to the northeast, since the winds of Cienfuegos are perpetually from the southwest — was a heavy wagon with a bed of two-inch planks, stout enough to bear the weight of six barrels of water, painfully hauled from the nearest pool for the horses of the grading crew. Beside it, a barrel sawed in halves served as water-trough. Bat's team was tied to the front wheels of the water-wagon.

Behind the chuck-wagon was a pit of mesquite coals, overhung by a long iron rack from which covered pots hung bubbling. A beanpot simmered over hot ashes at the pit corner, a giant's coffee-pot on another; a huge bake oven and its lid nested in the glowing coals, the lid first, the oven straddling on the lid for milder heating. George Walker, whistling, broad-shouldered, broad-browed, brown-bearded, extensively be-aproned, sleeves rolled up, was industrious at the chuck-box, building sour dough into bread. Cienfuegos held this truth to be self-evident, that all men were endowed with an inalienable right to hot bread three times a day. Hence the patient huddle of burros, gray or black or bear-colored, just out of chunking distance. They had seen the camp from afar and now waited for perquisites. By the custom of the country, cold biscuit would be theirs, late or soon.

Tham's ankles were skinned and Tham's heels were blistered. He hung his boots on the saddle-horn. A great relief to his poor feet, during the next riding time; much easier on the poor feet for the part of the next walking time. Then sand got into the broken blisters, sand tortured the raw ankles. The last drop of water was gone, miles and miles ago. The sun blazed down on gray sand, on red sand, on the white of alkali patches; there was no breath of moving air. Star Mountain, so far as the eye could tell, was no closer. Slow going, walking or riding; time lost to pull boots on over tortured feet, to pull boots off again from tortured and swollen feet; each way the worst. At the third walking spell, Tham slit the boots at the instep. At the fourth, he slit them over the toes and in the sides, cut out a round hole over each ankle bone, cut out the back of each boot to leave blistered heels free of leather, and thereafter made no poorer time afoot than when he rode Buck.

Tham's thoughts ran on water. Cold water, warm water, muddy water, clear water, sweet water, alkali water. He remembered cool springs under cliffs, swift streams that sparkled in the sun and gurgled over tree-roots, splashed on mossy boulders, foamed and flashed in cymbal clashing over staircase ledges. Roar of rivers in flood. Water dripping from overflowing railroad tanks. Water in irrigation ditches. Pools of rainwater. Blue of mountain lakes. Black water of sluggish prairie creeks. He had been spitting cotton for centuries, his lips were cracking. Wellsweeps and wooden pumps. Wellrope and wheel. Windmills, city faucets. Water in thin glasses on mahogany bars, water in tin dippers, water in pitchers, water in canteens, water in barrels. Water in oaken kegs. Water in a cedar bucket. Maybe that was best of all. Cedar buckets, white and red. And a drinking-gourd. That was best.

Limping, stumbling, staggering. 'We'll make it, Buck,' Tham croaked. 'My tongue ithen't beginning to thwell yet, and that old mountain ith thertainly clother than it wath.'

Buck's hollowed and glassy eyes were

lifted to Star Mountain, too. He did not know this country, but he knew what treasure mountains held; small streams and dear, that sunk and failed before they reached the desert. You could hardly call Buck beautiful, but not once did he drag back on the reins. 'Yeth thir, I can almoth thee where the thlope tharts up from the plain. Here ith where I ride a thpell.'

An hour later, Tham spoke to his pardner again, as they toiled up a small ground swell. 'Old boy, I thee a big thoapweed up on top and right there I'm going to hang up thith thaddle and thith gun, and dump thith dime in my pocket, and you and me, we'll be riding light.'

That dime was never dumped. For as they topped the rise, Tham saw, across the north, men and teams and wagons.

'God!' said Tham. He climbed painfully into the saddle. They turned to right angles to the trail. Then Buck saw what Tham had seen, and his little whinny meant exactly what Tham's little word had meant.

Buck stepped out bravely. Tham wiped grime of dust and sweat, some of it, from his face. He buckled on his gun-belt and straightened his humped shoulders.

Buck whinnied eagerly as they neared camp — a dusty, rusty tremble of a whinny. Tham hung the reins on a bush and limped a dozen steps to the wagon. The cook came to meet him, with a cup of cold water. The cook had been dry in his time.

'Gradual with that water, young fellow. Easy does it. All in?'

'Hell, no!' Tham's eyes were red-rimmed and swollen, his lips blood-stained, the wiry stubble on cheeks and chin caked with sweat and alkali dust. 'Thith ith pretty thoft. I wath expectin' to thaunter all the way to town. Money in the bank and chargeth paid.'

Walker's brown eyes crinkled pleasantly. 'I saw you inchin' along tol'able gradual, and I judged you'd pay us a call. So I put your name in the pot. Let you have one more cupful now. Then you sit down in the shade with Bat and wait awhile before you drink any more.'

Tham drank slowly and turned his eyes on Bat. He saw a large, thick, well-dressed man with a big expensive hat and a large, unsmiling face. The boss, probably. Tham spoke to both men.

'Gentlemen, I thee you haul your water — but can I get thome for my horth? There wath a dead cow in Magnethia Thpring, and that horth ith thuffering.'

Bat Cremony rose up scowling. 'Damn' likely! We have to feed every bum that comes along, I suppose, rag, tag, and bob-tail. But I'm not hauling water for other men's horses. Who are you, anyway? And how much reward is up for you? Them that comes in by Magnesia is mostly on the dodge, and if ever I saw the no-good label on any man's face, it's on yours.'

'Thomebody hath been writing you let-terth about me,' said Tham admiringly. 'No one could pothibly thith me up tho pat, juth from one look at me.' He pushed his hatbrim up and held it there; bloodshot eyes stared at Cremony.

'But you're makin' one mithtake, mither

deputy. Nobody ith ever going to pay you any money to bring me back — no plath, no time.' His hand fell slowly to scratch his chin, as if in some perplexity. It fell slowly to his side and rose as a man moves who treads on a rattlesnake. Cremony saw Tham's gun in Tham's hand and noted that the gun was cocked. 'Another mithtake ith to wear that thar on your cheth. It lookth juth like a target. The nexth mithtake wath that you ever wath born. It wath an acthident, I gueth.

'My horth, now, he ith going to drink your hauled water, and he ith going to drink it thlow, and he ith going to drink again. *Thut up!* And if you move a finger or thay juth one word —— *That mouth!* Clothe it! Let a horth thuffer, will you?'

The cook moved over to Cremony. The cook's eyes were dancing, and he held a stout length of mesquite root in his hands. 'As I understand it, stranger,' he said, 'you're forcing me to get Bat's gun? And if he makes one break, I'm to hit him over the head with this chunk? And then he's to

hook up his team and gradually leave us?
And I'm to watch him while he starts, so
you can water your horse undisturbed — is
that it? All right — but I want it distinctly
understood that I do it under compulsion,
under protest, in fear of my life. I don't
want to be shot protecting an overgrown,
nickel-chasing, white-livered, small-souled
this-and-that who wouldn't give water to a
starved horse.'

Buck drank and gave thanks to God and
Tham. Meanwhile, the cook chatted with
Bat Cremony as they harnessed Bat's team.

'You make out my time, Bat. After dinner, I'll tell Bernabel you said for him to
cook till you get another man down here. I
declare, Cremony, I hate to see you start
off this way, just at meal-time,' he said pleasantly. 'But, you see, if you was to stay, I
couldn't keep my dinner down. So you'd
better go. Come to think of it, the stranger
said you was to go. He's real convincing,
that stranger is. Cremony, when I first saw
you, I didn't like a hair of your head, and
I've gradually come to see that my first esti-

mate of you was too flattering. You've been
bullying this country for ten years. I'm
ashamed that it was left for a half-dead
stranger to be the first one to call you down.'

At this juncture, having tied Buck beyond the reach of too much water, Lithpin
Tham came around the water-wagon and
joined them. Cremony, disarmed, had now
no fear of being shot. He spoke up, snarl-
ing,

'You're going to be sorry for this!'

'Maybe tho, maybe tho,' said Tham and
fingered a lip. 'Then why not get it over?'
He drew his gun again. 'Mither,' said Tham
earnestly, 'thith ith the firth time I've been
right in any argument thinth I wath thix-
teen yearth old, and I feel right pleathed
with mythelf. I'm makin' the motht of it.
I may never get thutch a chanth again. You
go over to the water-wagon and grab the
top of a wheel with both handth. The front
wheel. Hold tight, till I thay different!'

Bat followed directions. Sweat ran down
his face, fearing he knew not what.

'Now, thir,' said Tham, addressing the

cook, 'will you oblige me tho far ath to buckle the gentlemanth gun on him again, jutht ath it wath?'

The cook complied with this request, and stepped back, interested. Tham went to the hind wheel, dropped his gun in the scabbard and clasped the rim with both hands. 'Mither Deputy,' he said gently, 'if you are dithpleathed with anything I've done, you've got an even break. Jutht turn yourthelf looth any time you feel like it.'

Silence. More silence. Bat held the wheel. Tham waited patiently for some time. 'I gueth that will be about all,' he said at last, stepping away. 'You go on up to town, Mither. Don't be uneathy about me. You're perfectly thafe, tho far ath I am contherned. I wouldn't thoot you for money in my hand. I'm a poor lot, I am — but tho long ath you're alive I can alwayth thay that there ith one four-fluther ith a thorryer thcamp than I am. Now you and your gun hop that buckboard and get further.'

'Stranger,' said the cook, 'my name is

Walker, George Walker, and I'm real glad to meet you.'

'I'm Tham Clark. They call me Lithpin Tham, for thome reathon or other. I wouldn't tell you thith, but thome thon of a theventh thon that knowth me will be thure to thow up and tell everything he ever heard.'

'Now I'll tell you what we'll do, Sam. You tuck a lot of good grub away, right now, before I call the boys in to dinner. Then tote my bed-roll over in the shade and tear off some sleep for yourself. I'll water your horse again and hang a nosebag on him, and then hobble him to nibble a few bites. After the boys eat, I'll take some cold biscuit and snare me two of the largest of these burros, and tie 'em up. About sunset, you and me will fork them two jacks, leading your horse, and we'll putter along to town. I'll not tell the Mexicans about how your horse was watered. They'd quit, and they're all owing money to Bat Cremony or to Jake Fowler. It would only make more trouble for them, and not do anybody any good.'

Shane McFarland and Bud rode rejoicing through the greenwood this day. Others of the spinning earth may have been merry, or gay, or wild with pride and delight; lovers in English lanes, weary folk in the peace of some island paradise, or youth triumphant in the shouting streets of the world's great places. Surely, Sam Clark was luckiest, happiest — who drank again, and sluiced down head and neck and arms and drank once more, and slept barefooted in the shade, his face on his bent arm. Again, Bucephalus was quite a horse, men say. But his best day was never like this day of Buck's.

CHAPTER VI

Oᴌᴅ houses long and low were razed to make room for

FOWLER, GENERAL MERCHANDISE

old trees cut down to let in the sunlight to

POST–OFFICE, DRY GOODS, GROCERIES BOOTS and SHOES, GENTS FURNISHINGS

The great store fronted the south upon the main street, at the southeast corner. Behind it, where once walled gardens were, stood now the eyeless bulk of a vast warehouse. An arching sign upon the gable announced:

J. H. FOWLER

Best Cash Price Paid for Hides and Wool

But that great warehouse was not all for hides and wool, nor half. These two in bulk were stored there against cool freighting months or waiting for higher market. But all the rear was given to baled alfalfa, tie-beam high, waiting for fat contracts at Army Post or Indian Reservation. There was slight but steady home use for alfalfa, too. Through the wide back doors of that warehouse unloaded wagons passed into a great wagon-yard, which, including blacksmith shop, took up all that was left of that unstinted and generous block. It was square, that wagon-yard, walled about by stalls and water-troughs and by clean bare rooms for campers, rooms never used except in storm or bitter cold. Campers preferred to bed down with neighbor stars for company, to cook by a common campfire, with careless sharing of resources and small tidbits. At the south-western corner, adjoining the blacksmith shop, the main gates fronted the outside world, and a lettered arch proclaimed

FREE WAGON–YARD AND CORRAL

Free. The stalls were free, the bedrooms free, even wood for your cooking was free. You paid only for hay and grain, and there was no time limit on your staying. Men had wintered there.

The free corral was identical in every respect with the caravanserai, the caravan-inn.

It is an old institution. In such a place, returning with corn from Egypt, Joseph's brethren opened their sacks for provender and found every man his money in the mouth of his sack, and their hearts failed them, and they were afraid. In such a place, to another Joseph, a son was born in Bethlehem.

This was the public wagon-yard. In his own private yard, a block back from the thoroughfare, Jake Fowler lodged his heavy freight outfits and his meager stage-line, small units of his army of occupation.

A large store, a mighty warehouse. But they did not quite fill up that side of the block. In the side street between store and warehouse, shut off from the corral by a high gateless wall, was a small patch of ground crowded with flowers and scented shrubbery, with vines and fruit trees. There, shaded and half-hidden, stood the one long, low room left unrazed from what once had been a long, low house. This was the private office of Jake Fowler.

'Good morning, sir.' Mr. Jake Fowler

glanced at the wall-clock as he rose from his desk. It was on the stroke of ten. 'You are punctual. Mr. — ah ——' He lifted a half-folded letter and glanced at it. 'Ah, yes. Mr. Hunter. Have a chair.' A slightly puzzled expression came to Mr. Fowler's pale blue eyes, and his brows arched, so that each pale blue eye became large and round, so that a broad circle of white showed about the iris. 'But haven't I seen you before, Mr. Hunter? I don't seem to remember.' A small line appeared on his smooth forehead.

'You have,' said Hunter. 'You wouldn't remember me. I was in working clothes then. Honest industry. Yes, yes.' His manner was brusque. Something, not in the words but in the tone, conveyed a thinly veiled insolence. Fowler's pale eyes hardened and the small lines on his forehead grew deeper. He looked down at the open letter in his hand.

'You speak here of business to discuss. To our mutual advantage, you say?'

'We will discuss that business,' said Mr. Hunter, 'when Bat Cremony arrives. I have no intention of going over the same ground twice.'

There was no mistake. Words, voice, and eye showed studied insolence, sneering and deliberate, not to be borne. The magnate took a step forward, with a stony face. Mr. Hunter leaned back in his chair and surveyed the magnate with an ironical eye. He saw a man of middle-size, straight and sturdy, well-knit, almost plump, short-fingered hands, and a roundish face — not an unpleasant face, except when engaged in professional stoniness, as at present. The mouth was too small.

'Young man,' said Fowler, sternly and slowly, 'will you be good enough to speak civilly when you speak to me?'

'I will do exactly as I please,' said Anson Hunter. 'Go back to your desk and sit down. Act like a busted flush.'

Mr. Fowler's ruddy cheeks became a few shades less ruddy. He was not a violent man and he did not like violent men. This singular visitor did not look in the least like a fighting man, when it came to that — yet such careless contempt was disconcerting. Mr. Fowler controlled himself with an effort. He went back to his desk. He sat down. A painful silence ensued. It was broken by Mr. Fowler, who said — not sternly:

'Cremony is not acquainted with the nature of your proposition, then?'

'He is not. Mr. Bat Cremony was peevish, not to say surly, at our meeting yesterday afternoon — when I woke up after a night on your alleged "stage." To be quite plain, Mr. Bat Cremony was in no condition for delicate negotiations. He was distinctly pickled. I told him to come over here at ten this morning and to come sober.'

'*You* told him? You told Bat Cremony what to do?' Again the magnate's eyes became round, broad white encircling pale iris.

'Exactly. By a singular coincidence, the gentleman is now turning in at your gate — which may answer your unspoken question.'

Cremony closed the door behind him and took a chair. 'Well, here I am,' he announced. 'Go on with the pig-stickin'. Or, if you insist on it, good mornin', of course.

To both of you. Yes — if I must be perse-
cuted by brutal cross-examination — it is no
kind of a morning at all, to me. It is the
morning after the day before to me.' He shot
a glance at the visitor. 'Hunter, if you found
me just a mite unreasonable, perhaps — and
pigheaded — that was whiskey speaking.'

'I found you unreasonable and pigheaded.
More than usual. That was partly the whiskey, doubtless.'

'That was yesterday,' said Cremony.

The deputy's face was puffy, but he was
sober. Mr. Fowler felt better. Mr. Fowler
was the mind, Cremony the arm. And the
eye which Cremony bent on Hunter was an
angry eye. Mr. Fowler felt considerably
better. He turned in his chair and looked
pointedly at the clock. 'Perhaps you will be
good enough to state your business, sir,' he
said coldly. 'Be brief, please. What was it
you wished to speak to us about?' He looked
at the clock again.

Mr. Hunter arose and sauntered over to
the clock. He opened it. He stopped the
pendulum. He closed the clock-face again,

and sauntered back to his chair. He sat down.

'I wish to speak of one hundred thousand dollars,' said Mr. Hunter. 'Probably more. Probably a hundred and fifty thousand. To be cut three ways. Have I your attention?'

Gone was Cremony's hostility. Fowler's offended dignity. Their faces lit up, they gave tongue together. Hunter held up a large hand to check them. A well-kept hand.

'Gentlemen, gentlemen! Fair and softly! There is no haste. Let me add, also, that there is no uncertainty. This money will surely be ours. But before I explain, let me stipulate, while it is fresh in your minds, that neither of you have the slightest guess as to where, why, and how, that I am the one who brings the most valuable contribution to our little confederacy. Knowledge. I bring you a fool-proof proposition, without uncertainty, without risk of failure, and without danger. It shall be yours to put it into effect. My modest stipulation is that my share shall be one third of the gross. I am to supply knowledge unshared by any man. Expense and effort are to be your contribution to the common good. Is it agreed?'

'Go on,' said Fowler.

'Is it agreed?'

'Yes,' said Fowler. 'Yes — if we decide to go through with it, your idea, after we hear what it is.'

'You will go through with it. I see it in your cold, greedy eyes. One third of the gross, Cremony?'

'I agree,' said Cremony. He licked his dry lips.

'You agree. One third of the gross to the true and only begetter. All is well. Gather around, brothers, and learn what you've missed. Don't bite yourself when you see what fools you've been. And don't interrupt. I am of a singularly amiable disposition,' said Mr. Hunter, 'but I don't like interruptions while I'm telling you what is what. I will supply all questions that hang trembling on your lips. And answer them.'

Cremony and Fowler leaned forward in their chairs to listen.

'You may perhaps remember that a short-cut railroad was once planned, to be called the Bee Line? I am assured you do, seeing how your simple and eager faces light up at the word. And you are wondering why it was never built, guessing, perhaps, that the needful money was hard to find. It is a wrong guess. Money was plentiful when the project was launched. We are now enjoying a time of panic, it is true. Yet it is a singular fact that there is exactly as much money in the country now as there was three years ago. All I would have to give for some of it would be my eye teeth and my heart's blood. But a railroad to cut off three hundred miles from the long haul — and with easier grades, besides — money could be found for that easily enough, even today. It was something else that was lacking.'

Fowler's eyes met Cremony's, each pair of eyes equally strained by a vast puzzlement.

'By your say, no lack of money to build with, no lack of freight to haul when built,' said Fowler gropingly. 'If that is a fact ——'

'You may take my say for the fact,' said Hunter. 'You have expressed the situation admirably. Plenty of money to build, plenty of freight to haul. Yet the road is not built. The answer?'

'To save my soul, I can't see any answer,' said Fowler.

'Make that two,' said Bat. 'I've suffered from chronic headache tryin' to cipher out why that road wasn't put through.'

'Give up?'

'Sure. What's the answer?'

'Water,' said Hunter.

CHAPTER VII

FOWLER stared. 'Water? What are you driving at? I don't get you.'

'No water to run a railroad with. Take your time. It will percolate.'

'Stuff and nonsense,' said Fowler. 'Aw, hell,' said the deputy sheriff; these remarks meaning, precisely translated, 'Oh, I beg your pardon, but really, you know ——'

'That's right, you're wrong again,' said Hunter. 'As you would doubtless remark, given time, there is no lack of small mountain streams to pipe down to the desert. Enough to run a dozen railroads. How true! But verily, dearly beloved, your water may do for what you class as human consumption, but it isn't fit for an engine boiler. It is foul with alkali, lime, soda, salt, copper, sulphur, and all the Latin names for them. It scales. It cakes. Boiler tubes are choked up — not after a while, but at once.

'The backers of the Bee Line didn't advertise their problems — wisely fearing to be held up for big money, big and double big, by owners of pure water. Their prudence was of no avail. For two hundred and sixty miles northeast to a given point — and for as far on each side of the right of way as you choose to mention, the Bee Line could find no supply of water fit to use in engines. Analysis of your water shows three degrees. The best is impossible; the next best is ———'

'I remember now,' said Cremony, 'that when I went up to Santa Rosa I heard about 'em boring wells all over the high country. But I thought that was just because there was no running water there.'

'Good water from up there could be piped down here by gravity,' said Hunter. 'Good water from here could be piped all the way to Santa Rosa, with pumping stations every few miles all the way up the hill. Expensive, but practical. There was no good water found. Each well worse than the others. Down here, at the very first, the Bee Line sent out trusted experts to get samples of all running water for analysis. Samples from every mile; samples from every mile for every month, in dry season and in flood. Samples from every spring and every well.

'These seekers, as you may well suppose, went about their investigations cautiously. Some, openly accredited representatives of the railroad, wandered about, ostensibly to look for possible freight, lumber, coal, tie-timber, ore rich enough to pay freight charges to the El Paso smelter. Water was what they sought for. And failed to find. Others, strangers, passed themselves off as well-to-do sportsmen, eager for good hunting; as archæ-ologists, digging in hill and valley to unearth the story of the Mimbreño tribes. One even went as a peddler. They all failed. Except one.'

Fowler rose and smote an open palm with a clenched fist. 'I place you now!' he said, in a roaring voice. 'You were a surveyor with the first crew. And you went hunting. Always hunting, odd times. Here, there, and yonder.'

'Right, my dear. The Bee Line rather humored my hobby for hunting. Right as rain. But why excite yourself? Cremony could

have told you that, any time. I rather culti-
vated Cremony from the first. You see, I
had known Cremony before, while I was still
a lad. In... Idaho, so to speak.' He turned
a merry eye on Cremony, whose face was
twisted with uneasy anger. 'Let us say, for
convenience, in Idaho. I have kept in touch
with Cremony for three years, and I sought
him out yesterday, to make sure he would be
with us on this joyful occasion.

'That brings us up to date. As you will
readily surmise, Mr. Fowler — none more
quickly — one of these trusted experts found
good water — and promptly betrayed the
hand that paid him. I was that traitor. So
much you will have surmised, knowing what
associates I have sought out for myself.'

So he said, languidly, with half-closed eyes,
goading these men with insult for his private
delight; the rich and powerful man, the
violent and dangerous man. Slur and taunt
and sneer passed unheeded. Eager, flushed,
alert, they had but one thought. Gold.

'It is true that promotion had passed me
by, most unfairly, more than once or twice.

I do not stress that fact. Had it been otherwise, I fancy that I would not have acted
differently. I kept my own counsel, knowing
that the value of my secret would be trebled
if the railroad people failed to find good water
elsewhere, confident that they would not.
They did not find that water. If I had tried
to cash in when I first made my discovery,
the best possible price must have been modest. The railroad fully expected to find good
water by boring, or to find some way to treat
the best of the obvious supply to make it
usable. I took that chance and waited,
suffering agonies of suspense for over three
years.'

He turned his eyes on Fowler: sparkling
eyes.

'I picked you for the front, Mr. Fowler.
Three years ago we would have been forced
to take the railroad's offer. Now you can
almost name your own price. This water is
their only chance, short of building another
railroad to haul water for this one. That is
not all. Better than another, you can hold
out for the maximum. It is known that you

are in no need of money. It follows that you can get four times as much as they would pay to a poor man. Myself, for instance.

'Why do I come to you? Easy. If I could handle the affair alone, I wouldn't be here. Cash is needed. I have no cash, and no means of raising it. Naturally. Being fool as well as scoundrel. Fowler, you have money, plenty of money. And I have studied your make-up, finding in you no touch of decency. I am, as you may have observed — well, to be harsh about it, what you see. My worst failing is that I have never posed as being a man of integrity and honor. It is a failing which you lack. You are evidently the man for my purpose. You rate one third of the gross, for which you will supply money needed to acquire title.

'Where does Bat come in? Bat's mission is to insure loyalty. I am not a killer. Suppose I had sought to make treaty with you alone, Mr. Fowler? Many things might have chanced, it is true. Theoretically. But only one outcome was possible in practice. You would pick my brains. Then you would double-cross me, and walk off with all the swag... So Bat draws down one third. You know Bat. You will not double-cross Bat. If you do, Bat will shoot you in the back, from ambush. You know it. So you will forego the double-crossing. I have never breathed a word of this to Bat. In this room and at this hour he first hears of it. But I had his usefulness in mind from the beginning. And yours. That is why I kept in touch with Bat.

'But what is to prevent you and Bat from doubling up upon me, and going halves? Here is no matter that I could take to court. I have considered that. I mentioned, did I not, the name of — Idaho? Was it Idaho, now? Be that as it may, I have taken my precautions. I keep in touch with — Idaho. If I fail to report, at certain set intervals of time, to a sure friend in — Idaho; or if any fatal mishap should befall me, prior to my safe return with my share of loot, and if word of that mishap reaches my friend — then a letter which I wrote long ago will be mailed in — Idaho. In which event, all the king's horses and all the king's men can't put Bat Cremony together again. I go unarmed, I sleep with my door unlocked, and I drink from every cup offered to me.

'There is a weakness to this arrangement. I admit it. If I should become the victim of a really-truly accident, an unarranged accident — that would be unlucky for Bat. He must take care of me.

'We are agreed, then, to be loyal conspirators, share and share alike? Surely. Here is the lay, then. The only soft water in all Cienfuegos is found in the intruded granite above Dorayme.'

The two La Huerta men groaned.

'In Olvidado. Bud Copeland's place. Young Copeland calls it High Dudgeon, I believe. The valley of Rest River. Plenty of water in Rest River — though the railroad will build a storage reservoir for rainy season surplus, of course. And the purest water in the territory, except Socorro water.

'Why didn't I go to young Copeland? Very high-spirited lad, young Copeland. Unquestioned integrity. Sure. Doubtless he would do the right thing by me. And then again, he might not... I have no hold on Copeland. But Bat will do what I want him to do, and you will do what Bat wants you to do. Simpler, surer. Aside from that, I have no great liking for what is called a "good" man. Some times I fancy that I am not a good man, myself. I seem to understand my own kind better.

'Enough said. Fowler, you hold a mortgage on the Copeland place. I have kept cases. It falls due shortly and it is hardly possible that Copeland can pay. So much Brother Bat's short and simple letters have told me, in rather sulky response to my artful queries. Not that I asked about High Dudgeon alone. Dear me, no! I asked questions about everybody.

'I have also kept in touch with all Bee Line activities. They have failed to find good water in wells. They have failed with a hundred attempts to treat water to make it fit for use. Most important of all, none of them have ever guessed that the unseen valley of Olvidado lay hidden above the high rimrock that walls in Dorayme. Any native could have told them — but no outsider would ever guess. They saw the headwaters of little Dorayme, a half-mile of staircase cliffs above, the central peak close over all. They heard of one rancher up there, saw a dim wagon-road on a ridge. They assumed a spring and passed it up. No indweller told them of a larger stream above the rimrock... Why should they? That was no news to in-dwellers. And no stranger would ever guess it. To strangers Dorayme wall was visibly the world's end.

'That was luck. Such luck will not hold forever. The rest is up to you. If you are stupid, you can wait for the mortgage to fall due, in the meantime taking such steps as your nature may suggest. Or, if you are wise, you will at once seek out Mr. Copeland, without finesse, and buy his ranch, paying him whatever is needful, over and above the mortgage, to get quick action. — Your play. And now I leave you. Don't be anxious, Cremony. I'll take good care of myself and avoid risks. My eye is fixed on Italy, and that dear Paris. I always wanted to go there. More than that, it is not probable that you will ever follow me to Europe. I sometimes suspect that you do not like me.

'Of course you will want to check up on Rest River water. Get it analyzed, and compare your analysis with standard and minimum requirements of railroads. That is a mere formality. You know, yourself, that Rest River water is the only soft water in three days' ride. You know that I would never accept such risks and take such pains unless I was sure of my ground.'

'I will have the analysis made, so I may speak with knowledge when I make my proposition to the railroad people,' said Fowler. 'But I will go to work on Copeland without waiting to hear from Denver. I have been a double-damned fool, but I can see the hole in a grindstone, once it is pointed out to me.'

Hunter rose. 'In that case, I hereby become a sleeping partner, as from this hour. This conspiracy has passed the whispering-together stage. I have whispered and now my whispering is all done. It is up to you. If you two execute as well as I have planned, you should get results with the least possible delay. It could not be said, truthfully, that I expect so much wisdom from you. With your limitations, it is to be expected that you will risk your sack of meal trying to dodge the toll. We shall see.'

He bowed gracefully and went whistling down the shaded walk.

'Well?' said Cremony, closing the door. 'What are you going to do? Buy Bud Copeland out?'

Fowler paced the floor. 'I'll make Bud just one offer. A good one. If he doesn't grab it ——' He left the sentence unfinished, cocked his head aslant, and turned an inquiring eye upon Cremony.

The deputy nodded. 'We'll fix him so he'll never pay off that mortgage. *What's that?* I'll fix him, you say? Don't you believe it. We'll fix him. That's what I said and that's what I mean. You're going to be in this as deep as I am. I'm done pulling chestnuts from the fire for you.'

'Cremony, you were sore about something yesterday. Otherwise, you would not have patronized your own bar so liberally. You never drink much except when you are peevish, you know. According to Hunter ——'

The deputy cursed long and loud.

'According to Hunter, you were ripe when he first saw you yesterday. Come, Bat — you and I can't afford to quarrel now. Too much at stake. What happened yesterday to set your teeth on edge? I didn't hear of anything.'

'Why, nothing much. A little private matter. Nothing to do with this water proposition. I'll toss yesterday's hand in the discard, and forget it. Lay off the booze, too. Say, isn't this the devil's own luck, to lose such a chance, right here in our own back yard — and to have to share with a rank outsider?' He broke off to a lurid description of the outsider, painstaking and eloquent.

'There's something to that.' Fowler nodded thoughtfully. 'Perhaps you are right. Couldn't we... get rid of him, Bat?' So said the merchant softly, with the same furtive and sidewise glance he had used before.

Cremony glared.

'Oh, well, you know best, of course. Yes. I heard what he said.' Fowler watched his colleague with a curious eye. 'Say, Bat — when he mentioned Idaho, did he mean Idaho? Or was Idaho just a symbol like x in the Algebra?'

'None of your damned business!' Cremony's great fist lacked little of crashing into the inquisitor's face; he checked himself with a visible effort. He flung through the door and slammed it violently.

Fowler sat long at his desk in thought. His face relaxed at last to a wintry smile. 'I wonder, now,' he said to himself, half-whispering. 'At least, it will do no harm to inquire, just in case.'

He consulted a wall map. At his desk he addressed an envelope: Sheriff's Office, Pocatello, Idaho. Opening a drawer, he took out a large envelope, filled with snapshots and photographs. One was a group photograph of a roundup crew. Bat Cremony was prominent in the foreground. With a sharp penknife, Mr. Fowler neatly removed the likeness of his accomplice. Next, he emptied his waste-paper basket into the little corner fireplace. Adding the mutilated photograph, he touched a match to the lot and watched until only ashes remained. Returning to his desk, he sought out a tablet of ruled paper — plain paper, lacking his printed letter-head. Thereon he wrote slowly, in awkward characters most unlike his own prim hand:

Gentlemen.
   Do any of the Idaho sheriffs want the man whose photograph is enclosed? If so, please communicate with me at La Huerta, giving details.

He hesitated for a moment before adding a signature. 'Yours, B. J. Lightwood.' Again the buttonhole mouth curved to a thin smile.

CHAPTER VIII

LITHPIN THAM sat in the whispering shade
before George Walker's little house. Tham
was all shaven and shorn, newly bathed,
attired in fresh garments of Walker's provid-
ing. His feet, unshod, tenderly bandaged,
rested on a second chair: at his elbow, a dish
of mellow apricots shared a third chair with
matches, tobacco, cigarette papers. The
smallest of *acequias* was backed up by the
smallest of all rock dams, and the little
splashing overflow made a small singing
there. Under the nearest tree of the near-by
pasture the Buck horse stood droop-hipped,
half-asleep and wholly content, from time to
time half-opening a drowsy eye. Crowded
fruit trees, vineyard gate, tall haystack in the
horseyard, all managed in some way to
blend with the little *'cequia* song, merry and
dear and old; the oldest song and the best,
with words unchanged since the beginning.
'Enough is all there is,' sang the little water
ditch.

George Walker rode in through the tangled

shade of cottonwood, willow, locust, and elm, bending his head at a low green archway; he dropped a new pair of soft and beaded moccasins by Tham's chair. He rode on to the horsepen, unsaddled and turned his horse into the pasture. Buck roused up and whinnied to his new friend.

'I didn't get you any boots.' George dispossessed the apricots, taking the chair for his own use; he rolled a cigarette. 'You don't want no boots till them feet of yours heal up, gradual. These *teguas*, now, they're two sizes too big. You favor your feet with them awhile. Time enough to buy your boots when we find you a job.'

'Fine,' said Tham. 'And maybe there won't be no job. I alwayth like to look on the bright thide of thingth. I wonder if you are counting on me to thend your money back, wonth I get away.'

'Better than that. Much better. I don't give a damn. You done earned this little, yesterday. I was sure entertained. Earned more than that, too. At least one little piece of money. You might want to buy some burning tobacco, or maybe to buy a drink or two for some of the boys, so as not to make yourself conspicuous. Ca'tridges, maybe.'

Sam fingered the new footgear awkwardly. 'Well, thir, I call that white of you.'

'Don't mention it. Listen now — you couldn't see for the trees, but when I went uptown I saw thunderheads peepin' over the hills, real earnest. Goin' to rain, sure as shootin' — maybe. High time. Coupla good gradual rains, three weeks for grass to grow. That means the general roundup and work for Sam Clark. I know the place for you. Bud Copeland, most of his cattle is right at home, but he's got some few scattered from hell to breakfast. He'll have to go to the work, and he'll be wanting someone to keep an eye on the ranch. That's you. Yes, and there'll be a little rail fence to hurl up. Maybe twenty mile, or some such. Soon as that fence is done, you won't have nothing much to do but ride around. Oh, cut and stack a little barley hay, maybe. About a month of that. You might hire me to help with the haying, if you feel like it. I don't have to go to the roundup. Every cow I got is right within ten mile of here. They don't know there is any other place than the Borachón.'

'While I'm waiting for rain — ithent there thomething I can do for you to thort of pay for my board?' Sam waved his hand toward the growing fields in explanation. 'Or ith thomebody workin' your plath on thareth?'

George grinned widely. 'Shares is right. I pay the taxes. Old Eusebio and his boys do what work is done, plowing, harvest, and *fatiga* work on the ditch. I furnish him work horses and whatever milk cows he needs. With alfalfa hay, they raise their calves better and bigger than if they was loose on the range, and still spare quite some milk for Eusebio. As to shares, I get all of my fruit I can eat, whatever milk, eggs, butter, and garden truck I need, besides pasture and hay for one, two, or more horses as the case may be. Eusebio gets the rest, and the cash for surplus, if any. He sells a few chickens, a little butter and eggs, a little alfalfa, a little wine — once in a while a little fruit. Doesn't work himself to death. No sense to it. Generally has more than he can sell. No market, much. Most folks raise their own. Nothing for you to do, you see.'

'And if you have long-time company, and an extra horth to feed?' Sam made this small suggestion thoughtfully, while he worried a bandaged foot into a moccasin. 'How doth Euthebio like that?'

''Sall right with Eusebio. Just as I do him a turn sometimes, or he hauls me a jag of wood when I need it.' George stopped for a little, happy laugh. 'Right nice place, La Huerta. This is one cozy corner where profit is not the main motive of life. Old Man Fowler, our local Shylock, he allowed to gobble some of these small gardens — letting the Mexicans get in debt to him, and then pouncing down on 'em. No luck at all. They stick together fine. They throw in together, a quarter here, a dollar there, five from some lucky guy. Many a mickle makes a muckle — and the little homestead is safe awhile. Maybe they steal a little when the collection is poor. I don't know. Coupla years back, Gregorio was about to lose his place, and our

big deputy rode up where Gregorio was
gradually butchering one of Tom Scott's
yearlin's. But Tom said he told Greg to kill
it and sell. Out of cash money on account of
a full hand, Tom said, and him ashamed to
peddle beef, so he had Gregorio do it for half.
Damned lie, I think. None of us like Fowler.
He's put too many people out of business.
Little storekeepers, freighters, three black-
smiths, one miller, one druggist. Undersell
them, break 'em. Then put up prices sky
high. Great scheme. Even set up a bigger
and better barber shop. We think he's in
cahoots with Cremony on the Oasis Saloon,
but we don't know it. Great on respectabil-
ity, Fowler is. Cremony does the dirty work,
mostly.'

'Oh, yeth, Mither Walker. That remindth
me. Do you thuppoth that deputy ithent
juth thatithfied?'

George considered. 'Ordinarily I would
say, *mucho cuidado!* But I think you've got
his number. Cremony showed up pretty poor
yesterday. No kind of a man, Cremony.
Just the same, he is plenty dangersome, once

powder really begins burning up, gradual. I wouldn't exactly call him yellow, all through. Point is, he hasn't got the particular kind of nerve needed to go in cold. I think you've got him buffaloed. Me siding you don't do no great harm, either. I am considered real stubborn.'

Sam Clark frowned. 'What thay we ride up after a thpell and thee how about it. You bein' along, I won't hardly be thcared at all. But I can't thand thuthpenth.'

'After dinner.'

'Dinner? We juth had breakfath.'

'Dinner,' repeated George firmly. 'Breakfast at ten o'clock. Two now. Four hours. Food is the biggest part of my diet and I make a habit of eating it.'

'Grub goeth. Got you by the foot. Oh, looky there, Mither Walker ——'

'Mister, my foot. George is the name. Look at what?'

Sam pointed through a gap overhead. 'Thee that cloud, will you? Fixing to rain, like you said. What thay I chop up a lot of wood and tote it in, while you thir up dinner?

Dry wood ith a heap of comfort when a thorm comes along.'

'Well, give your Buck horse another nose-bag of corn first. Mine too. Buck, he seems to be enjoyin' himself right smart. Gosh, if it really would rain, it would make us all a heap easier in our minds. It's some strain — waiting for the first rain. And when we get all set for a regular old he-rain, and it fools us — well, harder things are easier to bear than that. All of which is why I don't keep a lot of wood chopped up ahead. One reason, anyhow. Fellow would be willin' to build many a fire with wet wood to have rain to wet it with.'

'You know, Samuel,' said George, drying dishes, pipe in mouth, 'I judge maybe we'd better not strap on our guns when we amble along uptown. We don't wear guns in La Huerta much. This is the home town, sort of. Aside from that, Cremony, he'll be taking our little séance pretty hard. Holding a black grudge against us, sure. All the same, Bat will be most mighty anxious not to have this

story get out on him. If we go strutting uptown with our chests stuck out and all clut-
tered up with guns, it will look like a dare to
him, and also put him in mind that the law
don't let us tote guns in town, and that it is
strictly his business to see that we don't tote
guns. That gives him too much the advantage. But if he sees us meanderin' around,
noways hostile and without any guns, he'll
be wondering will we keep a shut mouth about
yesterday. I think he'll be glad to let the
matter drop. It would hurt Bat a heap to be
a laughing stock.'

Sam rinsed out the dishcloth and hung it
behind the stove. 'Yeth, and it would hurt
me, thort of, for him to thoot me up
thome.'

'Not a chance. It isn't done. Us people
here, our standards of conduct are what you
might call plenty flexible. All the same,
shooting down an unarmed man — this little
old town don't stand for that. Let's not have
any mistake. Guns or no guns, I never saw
the day I was afraid of Bat Cremony. Just
the same, I'm a heap less in danger from him

when my gun is hanging on the bedpost than I am when I've got it buckled on me.'

'Thuitth me,' said Sam. 'I'll try anything wonth. Leth go.'

George shook his head. 'Tarry a spell. Sit down and smoke a pipe for yourself. I sent Eusebio's oldest boy out to hunt up one of my sticks for you to ride. Your Buck horse, a little rest won't do him any harm.'

For a moment Lithpin Tham's leathern face lit up as a lantern glows. What he said was exactly nothing. He took a pipe from the mantel above the fireplace and cleaned it industriously.

'One thing you don't know, Sam. While you was laying down the law to Bat, yesterday, one of them Mexican teamsters, that Clovis — well, he came to the wagon to get a drink, and he saw the whole three-ring circus, him out of sight beyond the chuck-wagon and us three bein' considerable concentrated on our own affairs. He slipped back to work unbeknownst, and, for a wonder, he had sense enough not to say a word to the gang. They have a pretty thin time, them *paisanos*, and they can't very well afford to quarrel with their bread and butter. While you was asleep, after dinner, Clovis told me about it, and I bragged him up all sorts for bein' wise as Solomon. But when I went up-town this morning, there was Clovis, visibly intelligent, strutting around, all virtuous and swelled up. Seems he got to studyin' about Bat refusin' to give Buck any water, and he got madder and madder till he up and quit. Folks is funny, ain't they? I cautioned him again about not saying a word about our little ruckus yesterday — but I dunno, I dunno. Hello, here's the kid. That black horse next to the lead, that's your mount. Fat old scoundrel. Do him good to work a little. Come on, Sam. We'll sort of squander around and take a readin'.'

They rode up a narrow lane, under a green archway. Just where the lane came at right angles into the wide road, three horsemen whirled around the corner and met them at the lane's end. Three hasty horsemen, young-ish horsemen, angry horsemen, prominently belted and be-gunned. One carried a long-handled shovel. They reined up, scowling. The foremost swung his horse across the lane and cried out in a roaring voice:

'Turn back there, Walker; go back down the lane. We're going down to interview that damn' impudent Mex of yours. By gravy, he's going to heed what I tell him from now on.'

'Old Eusebio? What's he been and gone and done now?' said George, mildly curious.

'Damn you, are you backin' that Greaser up?'

'Probably I am. Nine chances in ten. You forget about Eusebio, for a minute, Strap. You listen to me. I got something for your personal attention. Listen close, because this is important. Don't you yell at me.'

'You telling me what I can do or can't do?'

The young man bawled this query, red-faced, louder than his opening roar.

'Exactly. You state the case with great clearness. I'm telling you you can't yell at me. I make a point of it. Conversation in a quieter tone or we call it a date, any time I've got a gun on me.'

'George is right, Strap,' said the second of

the newcomers. 'You got no call to bellow at George like that. George hasn't done anything.'

'That's better,' said George. 'Quiet being restored, we will first introduce my friend here in the moccasins, and then we'll look into Eusebio's case. Boys, this is Sam Clark. Sam, the peacemaker is Lant Stewart, the loud-mouthed guy is Strap Harrison, and the lad with the shovel is Henry Hall. And it's always fine weather when good fellows get together — if you will let me say as much in the interest of peace and long life. Look, it's going to rain, sure as cats a-fighting, almost, and we ought to be happy as thieves in a mill, every one of us. Silly to quarrel in the rainy season. I see a shovel and guess the same old story. What's eating you fellows? What's the row? And why all the guns?'

'Eusebio's been stealing water — that's what,' said Stewart.

'I don't *sabe*. None of you boys own any property in town.'

'My brother does,' said Lant Stewart. 'Your farmer cut off the water and I turned

it on again, peaceable. Then Eusebio changed
the ditch-gate back and we are going to
march him back up there and make him ——'

'Pardon, *señores!*' The interruption came
from a row of cherry trees beside the lane.
Eusebio stood in the gap there, ten feet from
the visiting horsemen; an old Mexican with
a thin beard, long and gray. He held a
double-barreled shotgun in his hands. Both
hammers were cocked and the muzzle adjusted to bear upon Strap Harrison's head.
'The *señores* are mistaken. They will not
make me cut off the water. This is the day
for me to take water from the ditch.'

'I was expecting this,' remarked George
tranquilly. 'That's why I baited you on to
bellow like a mad bull, Strap. I started the
debating society just to give Eusebio time to
do the rescue act.' So saying, he came close
and took Harrison's gun. He turned a smiling
face toward the other visitors. Simultane-
ously, the shotgun turned toward the other
visitors. Lithpin Tham warily made a circuit and relieved Stewart and Hall of their
heavy hardware.

'That will be all for today,' said Walker. His voice was pleasant and soothing. 'If 'Sebio had really been mistaken about the water, all Charlie had to do was to ride down and tell him. If Eusebio had a mind to act ugly, Charlie could then bring the ditch boss, paid to attend to precisely such disputes. Ditch boss would have turned the water where it belonged, and clapped a ten-dollar fine on Eusebio. Not to mention a storm a-comin' to water all fields. Fishy as hell. I'll bet these three guns of mine that Charlie has never heard the first word about it. I'll go up and ask him, right now, if you insist. There, there! You three be good boys. Run along and play. We'll be edging along. And maybe we'll study a spell, gradual, about how-come and what the big idea was.'

'But our guns,' said Henry Hall, plucking up courage. 'You can't do that to us!'

George Walker stared at him. 'Your guns? I don't understand you, Henry. Them guns are ours.'

CHAPTER IX

BUD and Shane took breakfast betimes and turned their backs on Olvidado when the first sun was crimson on the high snow above them. The hound followed them to the fence and looked on with troubled eyes as Bud let down the bars. Silver Dick, Bud's horse, turned to see; quite as if he understood. Bud took the black-and-tan head between his hands. 'You can't go, Mose. You stay here like a good old dog.' He gave that sorrowful head a small patting then, twisted a long ear, and put up the bars.

'He understood you, all right,' said Shane.

'Sure he understood me. I put out a lot of grub for him. About dusk tomorrow, if I'm not back, he'll go over to John's place. Second-best home for him. John likes to have him around.'

They looked back. The hound had gone to the top of a small knoll overlooking the little saddle where the road turned down to the desert. He sat up, skylined: he threw up his head in a bell-voiced howl.

Briskly through the red beds, briskly down the winding road, slowly down the zigzag trail, steep and double steep, that fell away into the triangle of Dorayme Pasture; down and down, past walnuts and unplowed fields, dying orchards and crumbling walls of old adobes, past locked church and empty store; down and down for ten miles to the farther gate — and still the desert levels were far below them. Once through the gate, the road turned leftward and followed the fence line, due south, at right angles with the drainage slopes, and climbing by stairstep ridges to a deep notch in the next star-point bastion. Slowly now, with banter and snatches of song, to that high-notched pass and over it into the broader triangle of the Borachón country; a straightaway at first, then angling upward across a hundred ridges and hollows to green La Huerta, high against the south. Thirty-five miles, early five to one o'clock, past, eight hours plus, four miles an hour and a bit over. Yet it was only twenty miles as the crow flies from Bud's gate to the first fields of La Huerta. That eight-hour road had duplicated the shape of the Big Dipper, the mountain high above them, the desert dim below.

They splashed through the Borachón, where the horses drank deep and came then to narrow fields and a network of ditches. Tall clouds towered above that mountain now, and men in the fields looked up to see; turning, in the nearer fields, with cheerful call or waved greeting for Bud and his friend. They came to the mother ditch and crossed on a high bridge to shaded streets, the multitudinous humming of bees and the long, drowsy town; came into a wider street, past church and school and little shops, past little eating-places and the one hotel; came at last to the great wagon-yard with the Oasis Saloon over against the wide gate, and the Fowler block beyond. Long hitchracks stood beside the Fowler store. Yet few wagons hitched there. Fowler got the trade, but in this place alone the great trees had been cleared away to make room for progress and plate glass. Teams and drivers liked the shade better, thank you.

Loud greetings for Tom Powers, the blacksmith, for Strong the yardmaster; stalls for
Silver Dick and bay Ben, corn in the feed-
box, a slice of baled alfalfa in the manger.
No unsaddling yet. The day was young.
They hung their guns and belts in the yard-
master's room. Spurs pleasantly a-jingle,
the two friends walked back to the nearest
restaurant to restore themselves with a light
lunch; beefsteak, chile and eggs, other trifles.
Three blocks back to the store, punctuated
by many halts for greetings from many
friends. Plump gray-haired Mrs. Redfield
held them up and rated Bud soundly. Why
didn't Bud and Shane come to her house to
stop, she hadn't seen Shane for three years
now, Jim would want to have a big talk over
old times. She spoke feelingly of straw-
berries and cream — and they would be twice
welcome. Bud pleaded business; Mrs. Redfield sniffed at this, plainly incredulous...
No, honest, Aunt Effie. Really business.
Sorry... Poker, probably?... Not a poke.
No booze, either. Next time, Aunt Effie.
It's a promise. Be up and see Jim before I go.

Gray-eyed Elsie Hamilton pounced joyfully upon the pair. Oh, Bud, are you going to stay for the dance? Saturday. Oh, please do! What day is this? Tuesday, silly!... Of course I remember Mr. McFarland. How could I help it? I practice that side-glance, Mr. Easy. Did I do it nicely? I think you might stay over, Bud — to please me. Why, Bud! You're positively blushing. What a lovely color. You know, if you played your cards just right, you might possibly take me. You can't? Oh, Bud — don't you like me any more?

'Shane,' said Bud, 'grab this little minx, will you, and hold her till I get a good start.'... (So began — 'another story.') Bud grumbled down the street. Business was a bore. Girls were a nuisance.

'Well, Mr. Fowler, I wandered down for a little chat with you about my faithful mortgage.'

Fowler sat at his desk in the private office. His face was warmly benignant. 'Pull up a chair, Bud, and tell me your troubles. This is the shop. When they have no troubles, I don't see them at all. Off they go, all over the map.'

Bud nodded. 'Yes. Like I did. Well, not to waste your time — what's the chance that the shop will let me renew my mortgage? Because there's a slim chance for me to take it up. You know that, of course. Here is how I'm fixed. A little more than a hundred and thirty steers to sell this fall. Some two's and three's held over. Dry cows to bring it up to a hundred and fifty, if you insist. Say eighteen hundred to cut down the principal. Yes, I can stretch a point and make it an even two thousand. That would leave three thousand due you.'

'And the interest for this year. Mustn't forget that, my boy — mustn't forget that.'

'And the interest. Well — can you let me make out a new mortgage for that much? For three years? — Prices are down to rock bottom now. They'll surely be up before three years.'

'So they said — three years ago,' observed Mr. Fowler brightly. His voice was cheerful, his small mouth curving to a small smile. 'Once and for all, I will not renew that mortgage.' He held up a small plump hand hastily. 'But I'm not going to squeeze you, either. Hold your horses and listen to a man old enough to be your father. What did you think I loaned you that money for, Bud?'

'For ten per cent, I hope,' said Bud. 'Ten per cent and good security.'

'Wrong. I can turn my money faster than that. Listen, my boy. I am going to be quite frank with you.'

Bud frowned. '"Frank" is a hateful word. It is always used to introduce something disagreeable.'

'Not this time, I hope. Not altogether. Bud, you've seen what I've done with Do-rayme. Did it ever occur to you that Olvidado would work in handy as summer range in connection with Dorayme?'

'Good Lord, Fowler! Haven't you got enough now?'

'Silly talk, boy. Childish. I saw how I could use Olvidado. And I saw that you were probably going to blow everything your father left you. So I let you have — what you asked for. If you paid up, well and good. If you were going to lose your ranch anyhow, I might as well have it as another. Better; it is worth more to me than to another. Now you come to me, saying you won't be able to lift the mortgage. If I choose, ranch and cattle are mine. No one else will buy. You know that. Too far out. Also, no money in stock, locally. Do I grab it?'

His face shone with benevolence, his voice was friendly and kind. 'Not a bit of it. I'll make you a generous offer, boy. Leave you so you can soon be on your feet again. Cattle sell at eight dollars. I'll allow you ten. Six thousand, if they tally out six hundred head; more or less as the tally runs. Over and above that, twenty-five hundred, cash in hand, for a deed to ranch and cattle. Eighty-five hundred dollars — more if you tally out over six hundred as we brand them. Five hundred dollars comes out of that, naturally, for interest due. How's that?'

'Thin,' said Bud. 'Ranch and cattle for

what the cattle ought to be worth —— Or, looking at it another way, ranch and cattle for less than the ranch is worth. Not to mention that you will be drawing down twenty-five hundred interest in all, on a loan of five thousand. You'll be getting my stuff for a net outlay of six thousand — one third of what it is worth.'

'At a forced sale? I think not.' Fowler's face was a shade less benevolent. 'Or, looking at it another way, I am making you a free gift of thirty-five hundred dollars out of good will — just to let you down easy.'

'I'll stick it out,' said Bud. 'You never can sometimes most always tell.'

Fowler rose up, and his eye was hard. 'One final offer. Five hundred more, and I'll throw off this year's interest. The mortgage and four thousand in cash for ranch and brand. Now or never.'

'Never,' said Bud. He rose to go. 'Well, so long. See you next November.'

Shane sat cross-legged on the sidewalk in the shade before Cremony's saloon, whittling industriously. Bud saw him there and crossed the street. A stranger sat on a pine bench beside Shane — a prosperous and youthful stranger with a handsome face, smiling as he talked. Laughter and scraps of tall talk floated out from that saloon. The loudest talk was Bat Cremony's, and Cremony's big white horse stood at ease under a tree. A known horse, Jumbo, and a good one.

'This is Mr. Hunter, Bud,' said Shane. 'Likewise, Mr. Hunter, this is Bud Copeland. Perhaps you two have met before. Mr. Hunter was a Bee Line surveyor.'

'No, we have never met. I went up to Olvidado on a hunting trip, Mr. Copeland, but you were away at the roundup. You had a man there, a Walter — somebody or other. Beautiful valley, that of yours, Mr. Copeland.'

'Here is a queer thing,' said Shane. 'My memory is good, as a general thing. But to save my soul I never can remember the proper way to introduce people — who to name first, and why. The big idea is to honor the stranger, of course — but I always lose the hang of it. Oh, well! It's no difference.'

'Good hunting up there now,' said Bud. 'Plenty deer. Come up and have a try. We'll make you comfortable.'

'No bear, I suppose?' Here Hunter's eye fell upon the mutilated hand.

Bud shook his head. 'No bear. I've got a hound now, and he ranges up and down, all over the shop, baying and following up scents and raising hell generally. Bears have no manner of use for a hound. Neither do mountain lions. They up and quit my range cold. Saves me many a calf and colt, old Mose does. Bears ain't so bad, but lions are sure hell on colts.'

Hunter's gaze clung to Bud's crippled hand, fascinated. Hunter's mouth opened and permitted words to roll out. 'How did you lose your fingers, Mr. Copeland?'

Bud held up his hand for one startled look. Then, on his face, surprise gave way to dismay. 'Dear me!' he said. 'I never noticed that before.'

An interruption came suddenly — not

unwelcome. Two horsemen turned the corner, dismounted, leaving their bridle reins adangle, and set sail for the saloon door.

'Well, if it isn't Gradual George!' said Shane, rising and pushing back his floppy hatbrim.

'Shane McFarland himself, in person,' said George. 'Come in, you and Bud and your friend. Have a drink and meet Sam, all of you. Reading from left to right — Sam Clark.'

They passed through the saloon door, still naming names. A shout greeted them from the bar; Bat Cremony, roaring joyfully.

'Come one, come all! The drinks are on me. Gather around and meet my new friend, there with Gradual George. I don't know his name yet. But listen to what he did to me yesterday, and made me like it.' He pounded the bar, and his great voice was hearty with laughter and jolly good-fellowship. 'Hear ye, hear ye! This is goin' to be good!

'Yesterday I was down to the camp, feeling real mean and cantankerous. I'd been drinking some. You fellows know me. Some days I'm not half-bad, but when I get to hitting the bottle, I'm just natchelly low-down and ugly. Along about noon, this man here comes riding in from over the flat, him and his horse in bad shape. Both of 'em needin' water, bad. And what do you suppose happened? You'd never guess, but I'll tell you.'

He told them. Fairly, accurately, fully, sparing himself not at all, punctuating the story with ungrudging and roaring laughter, till the room laughed with him. George and Sam looked at each other with a wild surmise.

'Gentlemen, that man will do to take along! That's the kind we need here. So far as I'm concerned, he gets the keys to the city, and he can have my star, too, any time he wants it. What's your friend's name, George?'

'Clark. Sam Clark.'

'Gentlemen,' cried Cremony, 'drink to Sam Clark. Bottoms up!'

'Bat, if that's the way you feel about it,'

said George, slowly and thoughtfully, 'maybe you might do a coupla little favors for me?'

'Sure will. Shoot!'

'By good rights, I should have packed my bed-roll up on a jack, last night,' said George. 'But I was feeling pretty crabbed myself, same as you, and I figured 'twould be a good idea to leave it, hoping you'd see your way to refuse to bring it up in a wagon. Lo and behold you, I was all wrong. First, you go straight on me, and next of all, here comes Bud and Shane and I want 'em to stay at my shack, and me shy of bedding.'

'Your bed is here now,' said Cremony. 'This morning I sent Florentino to take down a new cook, and told him to bring your roll back. What else?'

George hesitated. 'Well, I had to take three guns away from three of your handy men just now, and I was wondering how to get them guns back to their owners. Strap, and Henry Hall, and Lant. I was wondering would you turn the trick and maybe advise them some.'

'What was the big idea, George? I hadn't heard of any fuss. What was the trouble?'

'No trouble at all. They come pesticatin' around, r'aring for a fight. So I dehorned 'em. I left their guns with old Eusebio.'

'Look, George. I had nothing to do with this. What did they do?'

'It didn't get that far. They was strictly on the peck. Mentioned stealing Charlie's water, seems like, but that was just an excuse. Trouble was what they wanted. They got it.'

'I'll comb them down for fair,' said Cremony. Then he checked himself and an expression of bewildered puzzlement stole over his face. 'Be damned if I do! They heard about my run-in with Sam, here, maybe. And went out to get even for me. Blessed if I am not pleased and gratified. I didn't cut a very happy and gallant figure yesterday, as I remember it. I won't lie to you. If them three damned fools took it up for me, I'm glad of it.'

'Well, Eusebio will give you their guns, and when you hand 'em over, you advise

'em some. Any kind of advice. Suit yourself. Come on, Bud, you and Shane. It looks
like rain, more and more. Where'd you say
my bed was, Cremony? Over to Florentino's? Right. We'll go get it. So long,
everybody.'

Black clouds hid the summit of Star Mountain, lightning split that blackness with fiery
cracks; slowly, at first, then by brisk spurts,
steadily at last, the first rain came to La
Huerta. But four horses were safely sheltered
at Eusebio's before the first big drops fell;
their four masters had to run for it to reach
George's place dry shod. Lamplighting there
now, though it was early yet, for all the
world was dark with storm. Two fires there,
one where supper sang and chuckled and
hissed and sputtered on the stove, one in
the fireplace for fellowship and good cheer.
Laughter and much unnecessary talk — the
same subject being discussed in every house
within a hundred miles. This was the event
of the year, the first rain. Which will be
easier to understand if you will remember

that on some years the first rains never came.

'How about Cremony's war story, George?'

It was Bud who asked the question, when his coffee grinding was accomplished and he could once more hear his own voice.

'Well, sir, that's about as curious a thing as ever I come up against. Bud, he told the whole thing, from first to last, exactly as it happened. No excusin' himself, no touchin' lightly on parts which would have been mighty damaging to my self-love if such doings had been done by me, which I hope not. I'm free to say that if I had been narratin' that yarn on myself, I would have slurred some of those points.'

'That's easy. Saving his face,' said Shane, who was peeling potatoes. 'He was afraid you two would tell it on him. Beat you to it, and showed what a good sport he is. Clever. Good idea, and well carried out. Give him credit. Convincing — if I didn't happen to know better. How about you, Bud, how did you make out with your errand?'

'You'd never guess. I tackled Fowler about renewing my mortgage.'

'Hold on, Mither Copeland!' Sam held up a floury hand. 'I ain't conthidered truthworthy. I ain't conthidered rethpethable. Theemth like you ought to know that before you turn on the confidential.'

'A man is known by the company he keeps,' said Shane severely. 'Mr. Sam Clark, you're elected. We don't want to hear any more from you. Go on, Bud.'

'Well, that's funny, too. First of all, Fowler won't renew the mortgage.'

'You didn't think he would?' said George Walker.

'Then he went on and explained to me that he'd always wanted Olvidado. But,' said Bud, 'he next made haste to say that he didn't want to take advantage of me and he made me an offer, if I would close the deal right now. It lacked a hell of a lot of being a piker play, too, if anybody should drive up with a horse and carriage and ask you — considerin' that he practically has the immortal cinch on me. He offered me four thousand dollars over and above the mortgage ——'

'He — *what?*' said George. He rose hastily. 'There's a little whiskey left in a bottle, somewheres, if I can find it. You sit right still, Bud. I'll give you that, and you'll feel better.'

'Fact,' said Bud. 'I told him I'd tough it out. I sort of like that ranch myself. But that was his offer. Four thousand dollars cash in my grimy clutch. And throw off this year's interest, too. That's five hundred more. Said he needed the ranch, but he didn't want to cheat me.'

'"Smiling, the boy fell dead."' Shane rose up and his face was troubled. 'Cremony truthful, and Jake Fowler generous! I will prophesy with you for two bits a corner. Here is where the lion lies down on the lamb!'

CHAPTER X

THICK mist, whispering rain, driving rain, let-up or downpour, one after another, all the night through; and daylight brought a dripping fog, so dense and so clinging that no man might see the low treetops. Gutters were full, the roads were full, the fields flooded, the alfalfa swamped. Drip, drip, drip from the sodden trees; thunderous, swelling, sinking, changing the roar of the Borachón in flood. The fog lifted to a thin drizzle showing a black and heavy ceiling over all the desert, a ceiling level from hill to hill, a ceiling that twisted and crawled and writhed, but made no break in that black canopy. So Thursday went. But in the late afternoon, as the early dark came on, something befell for which there is no name.

You have heard, perhaps, the shrill shrieking of sirens, sudden alarm bells, the startling clamor of a hundred mill whistles shouting against each other, and shouting —PEACE! So, without warning or explanation, came

a mutter, a throbbing, an ominous drum-
ming, rising suddenly to a grinding roar,
from everywhere at once, echoed from cliff
and cloud, flooding the long desert leagues
with a whirlpool of terror and tortured
sound; horror, indistinguishable, mingled,
moaning, wailing, bellowing. The four we
know were no weaklings. Hard men — yet
their faces were pale enough now, before the
unknown and unguessable.

A cloudburst had fallen beyond the desert
upon the crest of the Infeliz Hills — so it was
learned, a week later. A cloudburst which
in one scant quarter of an hour had changed
a pleasant valley to a grim gash, seven miles
long, twenty to forty feet deep, three hundred yards wide. That great roar, penned
in by low, level clouds, echoing doubled and
redoubled from hill to hill, was the crash
and grinding of a million boulders wailing
together, tossed, falling, hurled forth again:
a million boulders, great and small, all at
once and altogether, floating, rolling, breaking, grinding each other to pebbles and sand,
a million boulders rushing down for a fall of

one third of a mile in the seven-mile down-
rush wash from hill to plain ... So night came
grim and black, in terror and in fear.

Friday broke to high, gray clouds, drifting
swiftly, and a slow, drenching downpour.
Noon saw the clouds driven in rout before a
bleak wind. Mid-afternoon saw the sun blaze
out upon clean-washed hills and a desert
that was half a sea. Sam went to town then
and bought boots and a slicker for himself.
And on Saturday, starting late and late,
that soaked roads might have time to dry
out, the four friends rode forth for Olvidado.
Their thought was that on the morrow Mc-
Farland and Walker would go up to Gallows
Hill, to a swift sale of the MC — the Shane
McFarland ranch and brand. To sacrifice
somewhat, if necessary, in order to get from
Clay Kinney, at the earliest day, an advance of so much of the purchase price as
would redeem the Sliding H mortgage.
Meantime, Sam was to stay with Bud. Those
two were to build fence, and other great
works, which Bud planned joyfully.

All this was not to be. They rode slowly

perforce, because of slippery roads and a hundred swales where horses broke through, fetlock deep, and because the soil of hill roads had washed away, leaving rubble for footing. Sunset fire and gold was upon them as they came to the Red Beds: and there, on every red hill and in every twisting valley, they saw red and white of the Sliding H cattle. Plainly, Bud's fence was down. Bud grumbled at that. Here would be a waste of time to comb the hills for those fool cows. Sunset was fading when they came to Bud's gate — and saw the heap of black and sodden ashes where Bud's house had been, scorched and shriveled trees bending above what had been a home.

Slipping, sliding, floundering in the dark through the soft rain-soaked valley of Rest River, toiling up the slow hogback to the summit, sliding down the breathless and breakneck trail that fell away to the east into a deep corkscrew canyon. Weary horses, poor Buck the weariest; late and late again when they won to the first wide place of that dark canyon, the ONO house and corrals, and a heartening warm glow at low windows.

Two dogs broke into a startled, frantic challenge. Bud was swift to note that there was no hound voice in that outcry, and he grumbled at the gate. 'Wouldn't that beat you? Where in hell has Mose gone to? *Hello, the house!*'

A wedge of light split the dark. John Marble was tall in the doorway, a tall stranger behind him; young Bill behind them both, tiptoe to crane over their shoulders. Bud led his horse into the shaft of light.

'Hello, John. Brought a few friends for supper. Only four of us.' The gate clicked shut behind him.

'Sure thing. Fetch a lantern, Bill.'

'John, have you seen anything of that worthless Mose?'

'Not a hair of him. You been gone?'

Bud's companions filed into the lane of light.

'Since Tuesday. Rain caught me in town and we laid over. Got back at sundown.

No more house than a road lizard. Lightning. Not a stick left.'

'Hell, Bud, that's tough luck.'

'Oh, I'll pull through, I guess,' said Bud cheerfully. 'Always have. Good neighbors, too — some of 'em. Here's where I lean. One saddle, one gun, one rope, and a pocket knife to set up housekeeping with. I'm a little worried about old Mose. He always comes over here, when I go away and stay.'

John Marble took the lighted lantern. 'Howdy, boys. Easy — Gradual — and one stranger. Welcome, all. We'll go and put up your horses while the boys knock up a little supper.'

Feed and good bedding for four tired horses. Perhaps a surreptitious slap or kind word for each of the four. The wide kitchen, all ablaze from a busy fireplace. No stove; the ONO was far beyond wagon-road hills and John Marble was a widower. Slim Bill Marble was the cook. Introductions, scamped over. Sam Clark knew no one at the ONO, the tall stranger knew none of the visitors. John Marble was forty-five,

fifty, iron-gray, weather-beaten, tall and
straight, broad-shouldered, narrow-hipped.
His booted feet were small for the bulk of
him. The tall stranger was even older than
Marble: vigorous, strong, and straight, with
a bold and spirited face, a shade less furrowed than any of the younger faces — ex-
cepting young Bill's. The stranger's eyes
were black and snapping.

'This is Dan Corby, boys,' said John
Marble. 'Dan Corby brought me up in
Bandera. Oh, yes, and Bill. Mr. Clark, this
is my boy Bill.'

Bill was slim, tow-headed, seventeen, joyous, eager, alert, silent. Of these seven, five
wore handle-bar mustaches of varying in-
tensities. Dan Corby's mustache was clipped,
and Dan Corby, broad-shouldered as any,
was just a trifle less tapering than the others
— exception made once more for Bill Marble, boyish and weedy, unformed. But seven
of the seven were bow-legged for cause; and
seven of the seven were friendly-faced. The
'folk' have a word for it: 'folksy.' It implies good-will to men. Not to be found in

dictionaries. The word is not in general use,
nor is that common which it names.

'Bud,' said John Marble, 'we'll make up
a pack-train bright and early, and we'll all
go over and hurl you up a shack, sudden
and soon.'

'You will not,' said Bud. 'Thanks, but
not yet. My fence is down and most of my
cattle are out. So I judge, anyhow, from
what I saw. The chances are that most of
'em are down on the flat by now. Can't see
why they all took a notion to pull out at the
same time, at once, or how they knew the
fence was down. If you'll come kindly,
we'll round up the coarsest of them cows
first of all. Stitch in time. You furnish grub
and bedding and cook outfit and I'll furnish
saddle-horses — and beef. We can take to
the barn if it rains again. Barn and workshop wasn't burned.'

John Marble and Dan Corby exchanged
glances. John was spokesman. 'We just
killed a beef. Remember that long-ear of
mine we tried to catch and wasted?
Brockle-faced one?'

'Sure I do. Following a line-back cow in the bunch with the old mossback steer.'

'That is her that Bill is cooking. Caught her in the open this morning, right in line with my rifle sights. Plenty beef, men, horses, grub, bedding, and time. We'll have a bee and barbecue later for the house-raising — but tomorrow we'll go over and bring your bossies. All except Bill. Poor Bill, he'll have to stay here and hold down the ONO.'

Then Bill spoke, for the first time, grieved, reproachful, eloquent.

'Hell, Dad!'

'I know, son. Make it up to you later. Someone's got to stay.' Later, while a merry clatter of knives and forks drew attention elsewhere, John Marble spoke aside with Bill in a guarded undertone. 'Son, if it was only working Bud's cows, I'd stay and let you go. But there's more to it than that. Old heads needed. Dan and me ain't sayin' nothing tonight, 'cause we want Bud to get his night's sleep. But it wasn't lightning that burned Bud's house. I'll tell him in the morning.'

He told him at breakfast.

'Bud, when did you see this wild bunch of mine last, the bunch this long ear was with?'

Bud reflected. 'Monday morning. Me and Shane tried to snare her.'

'Let me make a correction,' said Shane, smiling. 'What Bud means is that he tried to snare her. All I did was to try and figure out which way Bud had gone when I missed him. Here he was, and the next minute where was he?'

'Monday. And you went to town Tuesday. We saw her Tuesday, Dan and me. And we tried to catch her.'

'You tried,' murmured Dan Corby. 'I'm like Mr. McFarland. These damn' mountain men ——' He left the sentence unfinished, spreading his hand. Mountain men and plainsmen shared a laugh together.

'That heifer wasn't branded when we saw her Tuesday,' said John Marble. 'You went to town Tuesday. You got back last night. Bud, we killed that heifer yesterday because she was fresh branded. With your brand. Someone has been in Olvidado during the big rain — and branded that heifer to try to get you into trouble. More than one man — because they made a quick drive and shoved the bulk of your cattle, all they found in the open, out through the fence gap they had already made. My wild bunch saw the valley full of your cattle, streaking along and bawling. And, most likely, the wild bunch went hot foot to join the crowd. They do, you know. Get excited, lose their heads, just like men do. Follow the crowd, what's the row? And your friends saw that maverick of mine, saw a chance to do you dirt, branded her, and let the wild bunch go the first time they made a break. They'd try to break out, quick as they saw they'd made a big mistake... Somebody made a mistake when they branded that heifer. Only for that, we wouldn't have known. Somebody has got it in for you big and bad. Maybe they've made off with a bunch of your cattle. Not likely. Not likely at all. Who, where, and what could they do with them? Spite work, if you want my say.'

'Somebody has been sitting in your chair, Mr. Copeland,' said Dan Corby. 'Someone has slept in your bed and eaten from your bowl. Your house was not struck by lightning. It was burned down by men.'

Bud set his coffee-cup down and looked through the open window. His eyes sought the hilltops and held there, steadily. 'My dog is dead,' said Bud Copeland.

The ONO was a pack-saddle outfit. The horse pasture began at the corral gate. Pack-saddles, pack-horses, packers were plentiful; the pack-train, lacking nothing, was on the trail an hour by sun, the *remuda* of ONO saddle-horses following. Bud and his friends rode mounts borrowed from the ONO, and their tired horses of yesterday made the drag of today's horse herd. Forty miles of floundering through mud or slipsides was no fun. Especially for Buck, still road-weary. Bud rode alone to lead the pack-train, with a borrowed rifle and scabbard under his leg. Dan Corby rode in turn with each of the others, for earnest conversation. They saw a bunch of Bud's saddle-horses on the way, and threw them into the horse herd.

Pushing briskly, they reached Bud's place before ten, unpacking at the barn lot. They turned the *remuda* into the horse pasture.

'Sam,' said Bud, 'will you get dinner this time? We'll take turn and turn about with the cooking. Come with me, you boys. They've shot Mose and thrown him into the river.'

He led the way to the workshop. Under his direction they brought out a windlass with iron handles; something like a hundred and thirty feet of windlass rope, inch and a quarter; pick, shovel, two axes, hammer and spikes, a large wooden pulley block, a chain and two hardwood uprights of a windlass frame. All these, and three long pack-ropes besides, they carried to the upper lip of the box canyon nearly two hundred yards away, where Rest River, big in spate, plunged down into the dark in staircase cataracts. A silent procession, burdened and grieving. Bud chained the pulley to a stout tree overhanging the abyss; he passed one end of the windlass rope through the pulley, and made a loop. They cut two logs, with branches for spreaders

and braces; they set up and braced the uprights, spiking them to the log framework,
that framework braced against an outcrop
ledge of rock close beside the pulley; they
made the free end of the rope fast to the
windlass barrel and wound it home. Bud laid
his hat aside and walked to the verge. Then
John Marble said, raising his voice to be
heard in that roaring place:

'Bud, wouldn't it be better to let me go
down?'

Bud turned a bloodshot eye upon him.
'My dog, John. If I don't find him before
I get to the end of the windlass rope, then
you come down and bring all the pack-ropes.
With this hand of mine, I couldn't climb a
rope. But as far as I can go ——' He turned
his face away, and put his foot in the loop.
'He won't be far. I was down there once,
quite a ways, when I was a boy. Not
straight down. All rough and broken. Lots of
steps, like. Water hits a shelf and then jumps
off to the next step and so on. Let her go!'

They lowered him slowly, foot in loop,
hand clutching the rope. Forty feet down,

he was lost to sight in mist and spray. Once, twice, the rope went slack as Bud landed on a shelf and paused for search, then tightened again, as he swung off for the next drop. The rope unwound to the bitter end. Then it went slack. A muffled shout arose through the din of falling water. They wound up the windlass rope. John put by his hat and put his foot in the loop and so went down into the blackness, the coiled pack-ropes looped about a shoulder. A long wait then, twenty minutes or more. At last a shout reached them from the gloom below. They wound up. Bud swung himself to the rock wall as the windlass stopped. He was drenched, scratched, and bleeding. He nodded grimly. The rope went down again and came back with a lighter burden; poor Mose, slung in a cradle of pack-rope, soaked, shapeless, crushed, and pounded. Bud swung that burden in, loosened the sling and carried Mose beyond the tree that held the pulley, and took no pollution from that poor, crushed body. He beckoned to the windlass crew, and pointed with a finger of that crippled hand. They bent to see. Mose had been shot twice.

The windlass rope went down again to bring John Marble back to the sun. His face was masked with bloody mud, his hands bleeding, palm and back, his shirt was tattered rags, and his chest was scored across with a deep, angry scratch.

In silence, Bud doubled a pack-rope and made a second cradle, with loop and intertwined loop, half-stretcher and half-ladder. He looked up at John Marble. Together, they laid their dead friend in that cradle and bore him away. The others followed, carrying pick and shovel. Bud led them up through the gate to the little saddle, then to the knoll overlooking the pass — where Mose had said farewell. There, under a pleasant cedar, they gave him decent burial, silently. Each man carried a stone to lay upon the grave; and George Walker brought a second stone. 'For Sam,' said George Walker.

'Too late to go down to the flat today,' said Bud, after dinner. 'John, you take the boys and go down as far as the jump-off. Work back through the Red Beds and bring what cattle you find. I'll be patchin' up the fence. We'll be off to work the flat, tomorrow morning.'

It was an easy job to comb the Red Beds. They brought in something less than two hundred head, mostly of the weaker cattle, or cows with calves. They shoved them a mile or two beyond the camp. And as they came back, Dan Corby hung behind and spoke with Shane.

'Mr. McFarland, that Bud boy is taking it pretty hard about his dog. Unless I miss my guess, that man is ripe to do a piece of killing for himself. It's up to us not to give him any time to brood over it. All wrong to leave him here alone this afternoon. He should have been with the bunch.

'Now I aim to create a little diversion for his thoughts. Going to make a little talk, noisy talk, and declare myself in on this thing. If I should anger him, even — or at least get him to feeling a little crosswise at me, that wouldn't be such a bad thing at all.

He needs to have something to think of besides that dog. He'll get over his peeve by the time he hears me out. Sure, I know — I'm an outsider. I was, to be accurate. I packed a stone to that dog's grave, and now, by God, I'm one of the bunch.

'Butting in, yes. But I've got something to contribute. I have a pretty fair idea of how the land lies. Talked with all of you today. You told me more than anyone else, yourself. This man Cackleberry, he's intending to take Bud's ranch? And making sure he gets it? And you are figuring on a snap sale of your stuff to get Bud in the clear. That's what you said. Well, suppose the sale falls through. Might be a slip-up easy. Me, I'm going to show you how to pay off that mortgage this Fitzjaundice person holds over you — not soon but now. Check tonight. My check, with John Marble's endorsement. You don't know me from Adam, but John does. Don't worry about me, either. I'll not risk anything. I don't know you, but John Marble knows you.

'Three advantages. First, it will make this

ranch safe. And somebody is wanting this ranch a good deal more than I want it. Something back of all this dirty work. Something that none of us knows about. Dirtiest work I've seen or heard of yet, and I've been living in some salty communities. This unknown reason in proportion. You want to get that mortgage lifted, *pronto*.

'The second advantage is this. By your first plan, you would be going away to raise this money. It is in my mind that the best place for you is right beside your friend. Show-down may come any day, when you least expect it the most. And men that burn a house down will kill from ambush. You stick around. Third — and upon my soul, I believe this is most important of all — we'll be keeping Bud busy, hands and head. It is what he needs. He has a guess who killed his dog — not to mention who burned his house. A shrewd guess, I reckon. Just the same, it would be bad to shoot someone on guesswork. Therefore, right after supper, I shall raise up on my hind legs and discourse on the use and abuse of the guessing sticks.'

CHAPTER XI

'UNACCUSTOMED as I am ——' said Dan Corby. He said it very loud and clear. Five pairs of eyes turned upon him. He rose from his easeful seat on a bed-roll; he stood by the campfire and picked up the long running-iron which had doubled today as a poker, and with it drew a line in the sand. 'This line stands for something I intend to say, when I get around to it — something well worth while. I'm but a stranger here, but I'll leave it to John Marble. John, would I deceive this bunch with a false promise?'

'You harken and heed,' said John. He stuffed tobacco into his pipe. 'When Dan makes medicine, you take it. Every time.'

'Don't get me wrong,' said Dan Corby earnestly. 'All I claim is that when I get to that mark you will gain rather than lose to listen to me. Until I reach that line I promise nothing. And, with your kind permission, we will approach that goal gradually.' Keeping a wary eye upon that important line, he retreated to the opposite side of the fire.

'Here is a pretty kettle of fish,' he said. 'All you boys know this country and the people roundabout. I don't.'

'Neither do I,' said Sam.

'You've been here long enough to have yourself a hunch to play on,' said Corby. 'You told me so. Coming over this morning. I listened to this one and that one — until I think I have the situation sized up pretty well. What I would have you remark is that I have no previous knowledge, remembered or half-forgotten, on which to found a hunch. It follows that any contribution I make must be the product of pure reason. No impertinence or prying meant, Mr. Copeland ——'

'Bud,' said Bud. '*If* you please.'

'Bud, then. No prying meant, Bud — but no attempt has been made to hush-hush about the state of your affairs. Will it be O.K. if I state briefly what a fluent listener seems to think he heard — so you may correct me if my impression is wrong?'

'Shoot,' said Bud. 'We're not sensitive.

Or secretive, either. If it comes to that, when anybody begins getting real sly and cunning around here, we drop everything we're doing to look into the matter — just like we'd count what was left of the deck, and otherwise investigate, if we missed two or three aces. Shoot!'

'Short and sweet, then. You've got a fine chance to lose all your stuff, on a mortgage due shortly?... Right. And the holder of that mortgage, one Colonel Quackenbush, or similar, has made a surprisingly liberal offer to you?... Right. Which you declined with thanks?... Right. And Mr. McFarland — Shane, I mean — and Shane highly proposes to make a quick sale of his own stuff to get you out of hock?... Right. That brings us down to date.

'Your house is burned, your dog is killed, that heifer of John's branded to get you in trouble, if possible. And — something has happened to your cattle. Probable, at least possible, that a lot of your cattle have been run clear out of the country, under cover of the storm. Not one track left that was made before the storm. Once that storm started, ill-wishers could do safely what they would never dare in normal fair weather. Here are the three important points. Number One. Tracks. Number Two. A storm to wash out tracks. Number Three. The knowledge that the owner of Olvidado was stormbound in La Huerta... I will now take one short step toward the line which marks my worth-while remarks in the near future.'

He took that short step, cautiously, with a vigilant eye upon his goal; and then resumed his oratory.

'What do you boys do? You get out your guessing sticks. Fine. Guessing is a noble art, too much neglected. The skillful use of the guessing sticks is almost exactly the same process as triangulation. Guessing is a higher activity than reasoning. Granted. But guessing has one drawback. It is influenced by every hour of the guesser's past.

'What do the sticks say? They point to So-and-So — Fowler, the merchant prince, whose touch turns everything to gold. He

has been reaching out for Olvidado. Bud
has turned down his surprising offer. He
knows that Bud and Shane are in town.
Storm coming up. Lightning in the hills.
Here is his chance. Under cover of that storm,
merry hell can be raised at Olvidado. Enough
loss to Bud that he cannot possibly pay that
mortgage when it comes due, even if he sells
all his cows. Which implies that when we go
to look for Bud's cows tomorrow, we won't
find them all. Just to turn those cattle out
and make Bud a little trouble? — Slickers or
not, no one would ride all night in the rain,
and work all day in the rain, in double danger
and all discomfort, just for that. So the
guessing sticks say.

'Did Colonel Crœsus come himself? Not
at all. That's not Fowler's way. No man of
action. Hires all dirt done. Hires who? —
Not without a holdover memory of the world-
old firm of Business, Politics, and Crime, the
guessing sticks move over and take an
observation from another angle. Guessing
sticks point to Bat Cremony, deputy sheriff,
Fowler's right-hand man, half a partner, and

also, in his own right, a pedigreed this-and-that by birth, training, and inclination.'

George Walker nodded. 'I gave our orator that information, and I stand back of it. Cremony is a will-o'-the-wisp, net. Item, Friend Sam, here present, backed Cremony off the map. And next day Cremony gave him best, publicly. A fine thing to do, for some men. Bat Cremony never did a fine thing in his life. He didn't want to bother with Sam. Took his losses — because he had something on hand — something big. Olvidado was what he had in mind. And for help, he has hangers on, a-plenty. Some trifling men hereabouts.'

'If this was local talent,' said Corby, 'who was absent in the roll-call at La Huerta? Did you boys miss anybody?'

'We missed everybody,' said Shane. 'We holed up in George's house through the storm, and we didn't see a soul for two nights and two days, except George's man Friday, when he brought us milk and eggs and a couple of hens for the pot. But if any bunch of men have driven a mess of Bud's cattle clear out of the country, those men were missed last night. La Huerta pulled off a big dance last night. Everybody there except us. Bud was urged to stay over for it, too. I wanted to stay, myself, but Bud wouldn't wait.'

'A long time ago,' said Sam thoughtfully, 'cattle wath dithappearing, after a rain like thith, over wetht of the Mal Paith. Never wath theen or heard of. Then it wath whithpered about, ten yearth later, that them cattle wath hurried north up the middle of the flat, where nobody lived, then eatht about eighty mileth, and thold for five dollarth a head and no quethionth athked.'

'That is our case,' said Corby. 'What does Reason say, with no prejudice for or against any of the parties? Reason says, Why local talent? Why not a plain case of an outside gang and plain old-fashioned cow-stealing? — Because, gentlemen, it doesn't make sense. That's why. Stealing cattle is all very well. But cow-thieves do not work at their trade in such a storm as that. And when they did work at it, they'd take the whole bunch — not part of it. Cow-thieves might have burned Bud's house accidentally. But no outside cow-thief would have put Bud's brand on John's heifer. It doesn't make sense. And cow-thieves would never have killed Bud's dog. That dog was killed for spite. And those cattle were handled in that cold and bitter storm, not for what any man might gain, but for what Bud Copeland would lose.' He took an apprehensive step toward the waiting line which he had drawn in the sand.

'Reason turns back to local talent again. *Gentlemen, it doesn't make sense!* I've been around. The cattle business is shot. Your friend Fowler can get cattle for a song, a better ranch than this for less than he offered Bud. To say nothing of wages. Arson is high-priced. Stealing cattle by the day would come high. There has been an effort made to put Bud on the blink that is not justified by any reward in sight. There is something behind all this — something that we don't know anything about. And Bud's cattle? If La Huerta men drove part of Bud's cattle out of the country, those men will not be in La Huerta tonight. I will give odds of two to one that all your La Huerta people are present at that dance. Just the same, unless a bunch of Bud's cattle are missing, the whole business becomes sheer insanity. It was no child's play to drive those cattle. Ride all night in the storm, work all day in the storm, ride back to La Huerta the next night in the storm, a bullet or a rope if they got caught with the cattle, next thing to that if their absence is remarked upon. And all to make Bud a couple of days' work, in case his cattle are all hereabouts? It doesn't make sense. And yet, if the men that drove those cattle were not safe home to be counted when the storm blew over each one is a gone goose. That doesn't make sense.

'What to do next? Boys, I've lived in the cow country nearly all my life. I speak your language, mostly, except on state occasions. And I know your thoughts. What you think is this: We will now oil the guns and shoot it out — on a guess.

'I don't agree. Shooting it out on a guess

puts you too much at a disadvantage —
even when your guess is the right guess, as
at present. That is the way that decent men
become outlaws. Gentlemen, I use your
words, but I don't think your thoughts. I'm
a Yank. A Yank that was lucky enough to
have T.B. when he was a kid. I came early
here, but down in the bottom of my black
heart, I'm still a Yank. My thoughts run
on motives. The motive for most dirty work
is — greed. And this is just about the dirtiest
piece of work I've ever run up against.'

He planted himself firmly on the mark he
had made. 'There is only one thing clear
and plain in this business. Fowler and Company want this place, and they want it bad.
To get it, there is no violence they will not
do, no risk they will not take. I don't see
why — but there it is. They know why.
There is your motive. Greed. The thing to
do is, not to shoot someone, not even if you
shoot the right man. The thing to do is to
get this ranch out of hock. After that, we
can adjust other matters. Clear your ranch
first. This is where I shine. I propose, with-

out risk to myself or to you, to furnish the money to pay off that mortgage. And I propose to do it now — tonight and here. That was my thought when I made this mark and made a promise with it.'

'I'll say you've kept your promise,' said Bud. 'What I don't see is how you are going to play safe. Another mortgage? Go on: you interest me strangely.'

'No mortgage. Without risk to myself, I said. If things do not work out as I expect, I will have a modest profit for myself as well as safety. Trust a Yank for that. Here's the lay. If you agree, I'll write it out in the fewest possible words and we will all sign our John Hancocks to it, either as principals or as witnesses.

'McFarland, you expect to sell your brand to Clay Kinney, you said. And you told me your price. Ten dollars a head and you throw in your ranch. As it happens, I've ridden over a corner of your range and seen samples of your herd. I liked the looks of your cattle, and I didn't care much for your range. Like it better to be off by myself.

You had too many neighbors. Such as they were.

'As it happens, I am on the prowl to pick up a bunch of cattle, cheap. Just fool enough to think the price has touched bottom and that I can make money to buy now. But I had my eye on starting a ranch in a plumb new country. Never mind where. You'll be sorry when you see me sliding down our cellar door.

'Well and good. You want to sell quick. I want to buy, and have no objections to buying at once. Why can't we trade? Echo answers, trade. But there are small complications. Always are. You had intended to sell ranch and brand — and I don't want the ranch. True. But you need the money at once. Every man here knows why you need that money at once. To save Bud's place for him. Your place is just a well and a windmill to you, but this place is home to Bud. Wherever he goes, Olvidado will always be the center of the universe, for Bud. There is also a small matter of skullduggery as a factor. Item, you want to stay right here

for a while. Item, Clay Kinney will not want
to pay until the cattle are delivered into his
calloused palm. Item, Clay Kinney may
decide not to buy at all.

'How much do you need? Five thousand
cold. Plus interest for nine months. Plus a
working margin.'

'I have a little cash in the sock,' said Shane.
'Enough for a margin, what with our joint
credit and all.'

'You need ample margin. Can't have too
much,' said the unmoved benefactor cal-
lously. 'Here is what I will do, then, Mr.
Shane. I will advance eight times seven
hundred dollars to you. You expect to tally
out eight hundred head, and John says you
have them. Fifty-six hundred dollars advance against seven hundred head of cattle
from your brand, the MC. If the MC fails
to tally out seven hundred head, shortage
to be made good from ONO and Sliding H.
So agreed to by John and Bud over their
signatures.

'There's your cash. That agreement makes
me safe. In practice, if you can make your

proposed sale to Clay Kinney, go right along, making your contract read that he is to pay me fifty-five hundred dollars of the nefarious proceeds. How about it?'

'Yank,' said Shane, 'you've done bought a bunch of cattle. But we'll pay you your interest, of course.'

'Do you know,' said Corby, 'I do not think you will? This is not an investment that I'm making. I do not like such dirty work as has been going on here. You boys are going to take a fine fat chance for a bullet in your paunch, every one of you, to stop that dirty work. You'll not be paid for it. Such service is priceless. And it would be a queer thing if I were to take profit for the use of my money. As you may have noticed, I have safeguarded the principal. Besides, it is worth something to be boss, for one night. That's only fair, according to your own etiquette. Bud is boss here on his own range. Face up. If this same bunch of men crosses the divide to the ONO range, John Marble becomes boss, automatically, when you pass that so-called fence of Bud's. And when you leave the cow business and begin to project around with actual money, then you're on my range. Quite aside from all that, I have kept still for thirty-five years, and so I had a right to take the center of the stage tonight. I'll write out that contract, now, well contented. It will specify that if I have to buy your brand, I will pay eight dollars a head as long as you find them, and you are to keep the ranch. But if you make the other sale by November first, all I get is my money back.'

'Yank,' said Bud gravely, 'we will have to insist on one small thank you, I'm afraid. Not in public. Just between ourselves.'

'Write out your agreement,' said Shane. 'We'll sign it tomorrow morning to make it nice and legal. Today happens to be Sunday. Make your check tomorrow, too.'

'I'll give you a check, dear sir and Shane. You endorse it, then John, then Bud. Those three names ought to make it look good to Mortimer Moneybags. Yet he won't be pleased. He will not be pleased at all... Curiouser and curiouser!... Once more, Yanks and gentlemen, there is something behind all this sleight-of-hand and midnight murder — something that all our guessing sticks have never guessed out. All we know is that Fowler wants the Olvidado country — which means the Olvidado water. You make Olvidado safe. Then we all turn in and try to change our guesses into evidence, good in a court of law.'

CHAPTER XII

CATORCE PASTURE is eighteen miles by twelve, leased land. That means six townships, thirty-six square miles to a township. A sizable pasture, well stocked with sheep. Cienfuegos collectively refused to grant Cremony full ownership. A front for Fowler, said Cienfuegos; a partner, perhaps. Lease by township means something else as well. It means that the fence lines run due north and south, due east and west, as shown by the Government survey. The Olvidado crew had breakfast before day, saddled at first daylight, and reached the southeast corner of Catorce Pasture, just at the hill-foot end of Old Tom Copeland's corkscrew wagon-road, when that high corner was still in shadow, though the broad desert had long been flooded by sunlight.

At this corner the cow-hunt split. Bud, Gradual George and Sam rode west, downward to the desert. Shane, Dan Corby, and John rode north to work the eighteen miles of lane between fence and hill. That lane was a mile wide where the two crews parted. It was five miles wide where Shane turned back at the northeastern corner of Catorce Pasture. For the first ten or twelve miles they had seen Sliding H cattle in plenty: after that, none at all.

They turned back. Shane rode all the way to the mountain. No tracks going out since the rain. Then back toward the ranch, Shane at the hill-foot, John Marble in sight below him, Corby halfway between Marble and the fence. When they came to the first cattle, it was Shane's part to go up every little canyon as far as there were any tracks, and to rush those track-makers down to the open. That was the tradition: leader is to do the hardest work. John turned the running cattle to the south, they saw this third horseman coming and therefore kept their southward way. That meant that Shane and John had to do considerable to-and-fro work, at speed, to get their gatherings headed homeward; while Corby, purposely lagging a little, had only to make himself visible and to ride

straight on up that narrowing lane. At the
very last, Corby made one quick dash along
the fence until he got in front of the foremost
cattle, and then rode sedately in the lead to
the corner of the fence: so that the drifting
strings of cattle became a herd with Shane
on the uphill side, the fence on the west and
John Marble bringing up the rear. They had
caught close on two hundred head, with very
few steers. They reached the fence corner,
their starting-place, at about two in the
afternoon. This was where Bud was to
meet them. Bud was not there.

Bud's gang went down the steeper, shorter,
and wider lane that led to the west. They
saw a few cows with calves and a few old
cows, thin and weak, within the first five
miles. After that, nothing. They crossed
the wagon-road that led from Catorce head-
quarters to La Huerta. They turned the
corner of the pasture and rode north; they
made a wide circle into the desert, west to
the Mal Pais, and then south. No cattle;
no tracks. They bent to the southeast, then
wearily back to the lane again, finding no-

thing; they reached the waiting herd at four o'clock, bringing thirty-three head. Bud rode slowly around the herd, once and again, sizing up the catch. Then he beckoned to Corby and those two rode up the wagon-road in the lead, herd and herders following. Slowly, slowly, up the long hill: darkness close upon them as they passed the herd through the gate.

Supper was over. Bud threw on fresh wood and stood with his back to the fire.

'Well, we've brought back three hundred and fifty head, maybe more. Bulls, cows, and calves. Practically no steers. That makes it easy to reconstruct. Almost as if we were there.'

Shane turned his head to look at George Walker, arching a brow as a faint protest. George relayed that protest: it made the circle.

'I see,' said Bud, 'that I'll have to spell it. Here it is, then. They came up here Tuesday night and made a quick drive Wednesday, in the rain. They did not move my little bunch of mares, as you know. And it stands to reason that they didn't get many of the cattle in the roughs. Just what was easy to start. Say they left a hundred head in the brush. Seventy-five, if you like that better. Or a hundred and fifty. Yesterday and today we brought back more than three hundred and fifty, less than four hundred. No use counting them because we don't know how many they left in the Olvidado thickets. I had close to six hundred and fifty head in here, all told.

'All of which means that something from one hundred and fifty head to two hundred head are unaccounted for. Including nearly all of my steers and the strongest cows. Fat, barren cows. In other words, the stuff I intended to sell this fall.

'Here is what happened. They brought that quick drive through the fence about noon Wednesday, and gave them a shove down the hill. Then they high-tailed it down a side trail and waited. The strongest cattle got down the hill first — an automatic cut. I think there were four men in slickers. Not less than four tired men in slickers. Because one tired man rode west in the lead of that first bunch of steers and dry cows, west along the Catorce fence, and two tired men in slickers rode behind. They let what few weak cows there were drop out, and what few old cows there were — the little bunch I brought back this afternoon. They went on hell-for-leather with the rest. Where they went to, I don't know. That big rain washed out all tracks. And if ever I was sorry for a bunch of cow-thieves in my life, it is for those three or more thieves when that big rain struck them. Mind you, their horses were tired horses.'

'Grain for horses, grub for men. Grain-fed horses to start on. If you ask me,' said Shane, 'there was a fresh relay of men, outsiders, with fresh horses, that took those cattle and whirled them away north, while the original gang went back to town.'

'Maybe. Possible. I almost think not,' said Bud. 'How would they know when I was going to make a trip to town?'

'Maybe they were waiting for the chance,' Shane suggested. 'Waiting at the Catorce home ranch.'

'Not in a lifetime,' said George. 'Those Mex sheepherders of Bat's are decent *hombres*, every one. All raids based on Catorce are out of the question. No bunch of thieves would lay themselves wide open like that.' His eye twinkled. 'Shane, I am surprised. You speak like a man of small experience.'

'What's on your mind, Sam?' demanded Bud. 'Why that unhappy look?'

'Thympathy, like you thaid. For them poor wet waddyth. Partly that. Partly wondering. That outthide bunch — they might be waiting till you went to town. Man alwayth goeth to town, for tobacco. But it don't alwayth rain. A relay of cow-thievth waitin' for the firtht rain in New Mexico — they would thure need a heap of patienth.'

Shane grinned. 'That theory of mine doesn't stand investigation,' he agreed. 'Then, if there are no men missing in town, that vanished herd didn't go north. And I still think they went north. Now what, Sam? I give you right, and you look unhappier than ever.'

Sam evaded answer. 'Bud, you left one

tired man in a thlicker, thomewhereth. What became of him? He theemth to be the head man, giving orderth.'

'That head man stopped at the foot of the wagon-road and turned all cattle north,' said Bud. 'The cattle you brought in today, Shane. Then the big storm came on. You saw a hundred caves and overhangs coming up the hill. He stayed under a dry rock roof till the big storm was over. He was the boss. But arson is not a four-man job. Arson is a one-man job. No one left in the country. He knew he was safe. That night after the big storm stopped, he came back up here and burned my house. Mose charged him as he broke into the house. And he killed Mose. Then he went back to town... I am going to town tomorrow,' said Bud softly. 'To take Yank's check and lift my mortgage.'

'Hold everything!' said George Walker. 'I want to say some talk. I never had much of any schoolin' and I don't read hardly a-tall. But I listen, copious. And this very Shane McFarland as ever was, he told me once, half a lifetime ago, that the old Greeks used to have ten generals with their army, and one of 'em was the big boss, one day at a time, each one in his term. I just remembered that, gradual. Well Yank was boss yesterday. My turn now. I declare myself.

'Shane and me, we're supposed to be at Shane's ranch. Sam is supposed to be making fence for Bud. That's what we give out. Here is what this army does. Shane and Sam and me, we'll go back down to the flat and look some more for Bud's cattle and which way they went. Bud, you and John Marble hike yourselves to town, tomorrow. Take that check. Spring it on Fowler if circumstances force you. Otherwise, keep it in your pocket and say nothing. And for God's sake, hang up that damned gun of yours and forget about it. What we want to do is to find out more than we know now. And the very finest way to find out more than we know now is for you and John to wander around town, carefree and happy. Mix and mingle — not in big bunches, but one here and one there. And,' said George, 'if you do not say one single word to any man about your house

burning down, it is just possible that someone
will say a word to you about it. Kindly
sympathy.'

John Marble smote a fist into an open
palm and swore long and gratefully. Bud
pushed his hat back. His eyes danced in the
firelight. 'You just keep on being boss when
it comes my day, George. We'll try that
little thing. If anybody tips his hand ——'
Bud paused for thought. 'Why, then we
wander away from that man and quietly tell
a few people about my house. Then one or
two more, so it will get about quietly. Otherwise, the sympathetic gentlemen might notice
that it wasn't known about my house. That's
the stuff... After that, we do nothing, carefully, till we all get together and compare
notes. Shall we come back here, Gin'ral?'

'No. You stay down there till we come.
Always leaving that gun of yours on the
peg. Just enjoy yourself and listen to all
and sundry. You may not get any results.
I think you will. One man can keep a secret.
A gang of men never kept a secret yet....
That leaves you, Yank. Your part is to go

back to John's ranch and warn John's boy not to breathe one word to anyone about Bud's house being struck by lightning. If he has already seen someone and told 'em, then you high-tail it down to La Huerta and tell Bud. Otherwise, Bud may get some wrong ideas. You come on to La Huerta, anyhow, whether or no. We'll be needin' your head.'

'Mighty seldom that anybody comes our way,' said John Marble. 'Now, I want to make a suggestion. Shane, you write out a telegram to some friend in your town. Better address it to two or three friends, collectively. The first two might be gone on a *pasear*. Tell them to ride west and look for a herd of Sliding H stuff streaking it for parts unknown. Or any word or sign of a hasty herd. After all, there's a bunch of cattle gone. Bill can ride down to Fort Stanton and send your wire for you. A herd might go anywhere while the water-holes are full. West, east, or south, a herd would be seen. But for three or four days to northish, a herd would not be seen unless someone was looking for it, most particular. Nobody lives there.'

'Any objections, or suggestions?' demanded George. 'I hear none. It is so ordered. I think you might have given me a vote of thanks, like you did for Yank,' said George wistfully. 'Nemmine, it'll be Shane's turn tomorrow. See if he does as well as I did.'

'You remember all that wisdom I mentioned awhile ago? Mine? In spite of that,' said Bud thoughtfully, 'cattle might drift fifty miles before a storm, or twice fifty. Just walk away on their own legs. Sure. But they wouldn't go in one bunch. They'd scatter, and drop out, and we would find a few of 'em, here and there and other places. And they wouldn't burn down a house as they left. Not a chance for any mistake. Those cattle were encouraged to leave.'

CHAPTER XIII

THE outfit made a late start in the morning — or at least that half of the outfit which was to hunt for the missing cattle. Those three took each a blanket tightly rolled in a slicker and tied behind their saddles. They also carried with them a surprising quantity of cold beefsteak and cold bread. 'Because,' said George, 'we don't know where we'll wind up tonight, not within fifty miles.'

Bud, John, and Dan Corby were soon on their diverging ways, having no packs to make. Then Shane spoke up to his partners. 'I'd feel a heap easier in my mind if we had us a rifle apiece. Six-shooters are poor stuff to stop rustlers with. Umph! Bud's rifles all burned, his bedding, his clothes, all the jolly little contrivances Old Tom made, all the thousand trifles a man gathers in a lifetime. That's a tough piece of gristle to chaw. — Hi, Sam — what's the idea?'

'Thith horth ith barefooted behind,' said Sam. 'I'm goin' to tack thome thoes on.'

'Shucks, you don't need a shod horse on the flat.'

'We might leave the flat,' said Sam mildly, and proceeded with his horseshoeing. When that was accomplished, he filled a canteen and hung it on the saddle-horn. 'Water everywhere? Thure. Tankth and poolth anywhere. Rainwater, full of alkali and thalt. Thith is good water and I'm taking thome.'

After the late start, quiet riding brought them to the desert corner of the Catorce fence by nine in the morning. Shane turned north and George followed him. But Sam drew rein and called after them.

'I'm afraid I can't bring them cattle back by mythelf, not very handy,' he said. 'I wath hoping you'd come along to help me.'

'What's that?' His friends wheeled back to him. 'Sam Clark,' said Shane, 'have you been holding out on us?'

'Yeth. I told you I wathn't conthidered thafe. You athk anybody. They'll all tell you that Lithpin Tham ith no good. That ith why I know where them thievth took that bunch of cattle.' He pointed to the southwest.

'Out in the middle of the Mal Paith. Natural pathture. Plenty of bad water. Grath enough to keep that bunch a year. Ten feet of rock wall to put up acroth the trail, and Bud don't find them, and hith mortgage ith foreclothed on him.'

'Fiddler's Green!' said George. 'I've always heard that old yarn. Thought it was just a fairy tale, like all those hidden-treasure stories. We can all see the grass in there, of course. Big blob of it. Four or five miles across, looks like. But nobody has ever found any way to get in. A hundred have tried, one time and another — me, for one. Just like climbing over piles of broken beer bottles. I made a quarter of a mile, afoot, and like to never got out again. Wore out the soles of a good pair of boots. So that's why you shod your horse? Old Slyboots!'

'Why didn't you tell us yesterday?' Shane's voice had an edge to it.

'Leth ride,' said Sam. 'There ith a trail, and I know it. Why didn't I tell you yehtterday? It hath been a good many yearth thinth I left. Thomebody might have found that trail. I wath hoping maybe George or Bud knew about that plath. They didn't. Then I hoped thome of the others would know. *I* didn't want to be the one to tell.' He gave George a side-glance, half-comic and half-piteous. 'Eathy for you fellowth to talk. You've alwayth counted for a man, either one of you. But me, I been counted ath a full man for juth one week today. Thinth I locked hornth with that deputy theriff. I owed mythelf the chanth that thome other man would lead Bud to them cattle. From now on, I'll be a minuth perthon, again. I could thue mythelf for damageth, and win the cath.'

They rode beside him. 'Sam, my son,' said George judicially, 'I think you'll rank as a plus person for a while yet, far as I can see. Looking back, real careful, I seem to remember quite a spell when I wasn't any especial credit to my bringin' up. How about you, Shane? Did your halo bruise your head any, at first? Or did you always have it?'

'My halo is a comparatively recent acquisition,' said Shane gravely. 'You cheer

up, Sam. We're all with you. Lead us to
your trail. Not but what it is mostly a
formality. Of course, Bud's stuff is there.
It couldn't be any other way. "By the con-
ditions of the problem" — as the teacher
used to say. Is it far, Sam?'

'Not in mileth. But it ith the damnedeth
one trail you ever thaw.'

They came to thin red sand, to thin gray
sand, to white gyp country, to the high black
wall of the Mal Pais, angling across the
plain toward the southwest. They turned
southwest with it. Water-courses ran beside
the lava flow, with deep holes gouged out.
each hole a pool of flood water, brown or
yellow. An hour beside the Mal Pais, twice
riding wide where deep alluvial soil, washed
down from the hills, had piled against the
lava wall, so that vegetation had made a
tangled and thorny jungle there.

'This trail of yours — is it marked out
any way?' asked George. 'Little rock piles,
or the like? Scratches on the rock?'

'No. They dathent make monumenth and
none wath needed. Onth you get tharted

right, there ain't no way to get off that trail.
It went the only way a horth could go, and
that wath twithty. You loop about rock
pilth and broken bubbleth, half a mile to
make two hundred yardth. You'll thee.'

They saw. Sam rode slower, halting to
look back and take his bearings. He lined
up two peaks at last, turned up a twisting
inlet, one of a score of such inlets. Following
the narrow gully they saw the first sign of
that vanished herd. There had been no
tracks. That heavy rain had wiped the slate
clean. But in this narrow place the stunted
bushes were crushed and broken, freshly so;
the herd had passed this way. The gully
ended in a blank wall, but there was a slop-
ing shelf which led away to the right. Sam
pointed to that shelf, to fresh white scratches
on the black lava.

'Horseshoes,' said Shane.

They climbed that drooping shelf and
came to a weird tableland of lava, incredibly
rough and broken, as if the sea in storm had
turned to rock, that tumult fixed forever.
For most part, the broken lava was like no-

thing so much as sponges of black glass, edged
like a knife for sharpness. But there was a
twisting way of unbroken lava, the edges
blunted by sandstorms of unnumbered centuries, so that a horse might walk there at a
creeping pace; a way now wide, now narrow,
sometimes steep, always crooked; skirting
dreadful pits, where white-hot bubbles had
broken; twisting between windrows of broken
rock; a dreadful maze, looping, turning, crawl-
ing, dodging by hollow and by hill. And at
one gnarled hill, Sam dismounted.

'Thoth fellowth, they ain't here, of courth,'
said Sam sagely. 'But if they wath here with
rifleth, we'd look real thilly, riding up on
them. We'll walk.'

They walked. Shunning the skyline, bent
low, keeping cover; came to where they
could see the wide pasture lands open up
before them, red and white with many cattle.
Some were close below them; so close that
they could see the brand, the Sliding H.
They came at last to a wall of lava rocks,
freshly builded, across the trail. They sat
down here to rest.

'No cowhands,' said George. 'I knew there wouldn't be, but I love to crawl on this sharp rock. Good for the hands and knees.'

'That is that,' said Shane. 'Noon. We rode slow and steady. With fresh, strong cattle, pushing without any regard for consequences, with the fear of death at their heels, those fellows could just about make it here before that biggest storm broke, Thursday.'

'There ith a cave down there,' said Sam. 'One of thoth bubbleth, with one thide broke out. Big enough for them and their hortheth.'

Shane nodded. 'They could take shelter there till the worst of the storm was over, about midnight, and then go back to town. Twelve hours of rain after that, enough to wash out all tracks. I don't envy them. Tired men, tired horses. We'll be tired ourselves, when we get in, and we rode on dry ground, with a light conscience. How far is it to town, George?'

'Thirty miles. Thirty-five. Maybe they didn't have to go all the way back to town. Strap Harrison's little old ranch is ten miles this side. If it was Strap, now, he wouldn't have to go so far. That's a good bet. Strap and Hall and Stewart. Always together, three of a kind — Bat's men, and them sore at me and all my friends... Shucks!... Well, those cattle are doing fine, right where they are. We'll leave them there, and we will now go to town and tell Bud the news, and put all our wise heads together. Let's drift.'

'Wait a minute,' said Shane. He produced a jack-knife. The big blade was broken short. With that broken blade he scratched boldly on the smoothest stone in the wall across the trail. This is what he made there; the Sliding H:

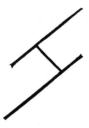

They mounted and crept back along that crooked trail to the open plain. They ate their lunch then and drank from Sam's canteen, and smoked, while their horses cropped the short grasses there. Then they struck out across the trackless waste in a bee line for La Huerta, high above them, a smudge of green moss on a far-away slope.

CHAPTER XIV

'FRIENDS, farmers, freemen! That rain was one joyous affair for Cienfuegos. High up as I am, I had pretty plenty of grass yet, but down toward the flat, it was most mighty short. And out on the flat — oh, man! I was out there two weeks ago, out in front of Moonshine, lookin' for that fool Jig horse of mine. Made a twenty-mile circle, and I'll tell you true; in all that twenty miles, if you had taken a pair of tweezers and pulled all the grass I saw, roots and all, you wouldn't have found enough to make a tooth-brush. Different now. Greening up in the foothills already, grass on the flats in two or three weeks. No more cows dyin' off on us, more rains to come. Roundup next month, steers to sell, debts to pay — bully! After my debts are paid, if my credit's good, then I'm goin' to give a dance. I missed this one. Was it a good one, Ed?'

Bud was the speaker. He was fresh from the barber's hands, shaven and shorn, glo-

rious with bay rum. John Marble was in
the chair now. These two came late to La
Huerta. After a small late lunch at Pete's
Place, the two friends had started on a loitering progress along the business street, chat-
ting largely with wagon-master, blacksmith,
clerk, barber, and passer-by. Bud's joyous
remarks were addressed to Ed Little, who
was 'next' — Big Ed Little from Los Genios.

'Best I ever see,' said Ed. 'Everybody
gay, on account of the rain, like you. No
drinkin', no fightin'. Grandma Edwards and
old man Shaw, they stood up and pranced
through the Virginny Reel like two colts.
Yes, they did. You missed something, cowboy. Everybody here but you. Old Stony
Face, there' — Ed jerked his chin to indi-
cate that the much be-lathered Marble, in
the chair, was Old Stony Face — 'why, he
trades at the Fort, and we seldom see him
down this way. But everyone else was here
but you — lumber-jacks from the mill, min-
ers, everybody. Young Lant Stewart, he
was the belle of the ball — all dicked up like
a red wagon. Young stranger too — Hunter,

his name was — he made a big hit with the
girls. Stage-driver wasn't there, either. Mail
didn't get through till this morning. Just
one big swamp beyond Guffy's Well, Slim
says. And Gradual George, he's lit out for
a job of work, they tell me. Gallows Hill
way, somewhere. But George, he's not much
of a ladies' man. George is what you might
call an old bachelor, and some set in his
ways. George wasn't missed so much. Not
like you. I heard a heap of complaints about
you. Don't know that I ever saw you lookin'
so peart, either. Bright and sparkling. Them
young things are sure goin' to jaw you about
missin' that dance, I'll tell you that.'

'Had to go, Ed. My roof leaks, and I was
scared my bedding and so on would be
spoiled. I'm tol'able trifling, seems like,'
said Bud. 'I oughta fixed that roof a month
ago.'

The doctor came in and chatted. Harry
Moore came in and chatted; not joyfully.
Harry had a grievance.

'Bat Cremony is dealing out misery again.
Serving papers right and left. I've got to

serve on the grand jury. And court sets at roundup time always, spring and fall. Roundup time for stockmen, seedtime and harvest for the farmers. Wouldn't you think they'd have sense enough to hold court between times? This cripples us. If you're not being tried for something, you're subpœnaed as a witness, or else you're a juryman. And Bat, he gets ten cents a mile, going and coming, for every warrant or summons. Highway robbery, that is. Sackful of 'em came in the mail today. Two cents postage brings 'em from Cibola to La Huerta, and every paper that Bat serves costs the county eighteen dollars, besides the mileage from here on.'

The doctor sympathized with these views at some length. But Moore was still eloquent when John Marble stepped down from the barber's chair. The two friends sauntered down the street.

'Bud, you look as happy as a cow in a clover patch,' said John. 'That was a bright idea of yours, to sing and laugh coming down, for practice. Nobody expects much

from me, Old Stony Face — but you're one
of the twinkle-eye tribe. I was afraid you
couldn't do it. But a body would think,
looking at you, that you hadn't a care on
earth. What do we do now?'

'Shine some more,' said Bud. 'Saloon
next. Gang hasn't gathered yet, but that is
the place. On the face of the returns, all
La Huerta men showed up at that *baile*.
Leastways, I've heard every name mentioned
that could possibly fall under suspicion.'

'That's what we expected. Nobody seems
to have heard about your fire yet, either.
After supper, and a few drinks, we may hear
something new.'

There was one game of solo in the Oasis,
and one five-handed game of pitch. John
made it six-handed. Bud bought a round of
drinks. Then he wandered down the street,
past Fowler's store, past the hotel, past the
little Mexican store, past butcher and baker;
gossiping with all comers. When that lei-
surely stroll brought him back to the Oasis,
the pitch game had broken up. Bud and
John brought chairs out to the pleasant

shade of the sidewalk, in front of the saloon;
they leaned back luxuriously there, smoking, a picture of careless content, with jest
or waved greeting for every passer-by. Anson Hunter came down the opposite side of
the street, carrying a book. He saw Bud
and crossed over.

'That was hard luck about your house,
Mr. Copeland.'

'Sure was,' said Bud. 'Damn the lightning, anyhow.' Then he shrugged his shoulders and looked up with smiling eyes. 'Oh,
I'll make out. Bachelor can always make
out, somehow. I lost considerable plunder,
of course, but the house wasn't so much.
Plenty of logs in Olvidado. The boys will
get together and hurl me up another house
when I'm ready. Have a bee and a barbecue. Dance, maybe. I'm going up to the
mill tomorrow and pick out a bill of lumber
for floors, doors, frames, and such. Knock
up tables and bunk and benches. Bought
me a mess of second-hand windows and
frames today, from an old abandoned adobe,
here in town. I'll make out, fine. Oh, ex-

cuse me, Mr. Hunter. You haven't met my friend, have you?'

Introductions were made and acknowledged. Bud gave his chair to Hunter, who took it under protest. Bud sat cross-legged on the sidewalk and rolled himself a smoke.

'John is my next-door neighbor, Mr. Hunter. Ten miles. He staked me to a bed and a camp outfit, and I'm living in my workshop. Say, that reminds me. That deer hunt, you know ——' Bud paused, embarrassed.

'Oh, we'll call that off, of course,' said Hunter. 'That says itself. You'll be too busy to bother with me.'

'Come up to my place,' said Marble. 'Not near so sightly as Bud's ranch, but you're welcome. Ride up with me tomorrow.'

'Thank you,' said Hunter. 'Later, perhaps. I promised to go up to the mill, this week. Mr. Price thought we might find a bear up there.'

'Any time you're ready, come on up,' said John. 'I'm always there. My son goes to the roundup for me. You boys excuse me, will you? I've got to get a letter in the post-office. Just remembered it.'

He went to the post-office; made casual mention there that lightning had struck Bud's house and burned it to the ground. He came back by way of the wagon-yard and mentioned Bud's house there. Why didn't you tell us that awhile ago? Oh, we hated to, sort of. Everybody was feeling jolly, and it seemed a shame to spring bad news on you. I'll do hinges and bolts, hooks and hangers and the like o' that, said the blacksmith. Speaking for Bud, I'll take you up on that, fair sir and mister, thank you kindly, sir, she said.

Sure now that this word would spread, John came back to the Oasis. Hunter and Bud were smoking cigars now, and Bud was telling old tales anew. John took a cigar and took part in those old tales. The Oldest Road: the Lincoln County War: the Old Salt Road: Victorio, Juh, Geronimo. Passing citizens paused to assure Bud of their sympathy. Last of all, Bat Cremony broke in on that story-telling. White Jumbo came reach-foot down the street; Cremony swung off and stepped up on the walk. Deep concern was on his face and in his voice.

'What's this they're telling me, Copeland? The blacksmith says your house burned up.'

'Yes,' said Bud. He pushed his hatbrim back and stretched his arms, with a little yawn. 'No more house than a road lizard. Lightning hit her.'

'Ain't that hell? Look, Bud. You go down to Catorce. There's a bully good tent there. You tell Ramon I said for you to take it. Anything else you want. Pots and pans, Dutch oven, axe? Help yourself.'

'You're too late, Bat. Thank you, just the same. Don't need a tent. I'm holed up in my workshop. That didn't burn.'

'Haystack? Stable?' Cremony's voice was anxious. 'Did they burn?'

'Neither one of them. Just the house. And John brought over everything I need. Most of my cattle are down at your place, though — eating the grass between your fence and the mountains. They broke my fence down, during the storm. If you don't mind, I'll let them stay down there a spell, till I get organized. They'll begin coming back, anyway, soon as the surface water dries up. And I'm middling busy, just now.'

'Let 'em stay as long as you like,' said Bat heartily. 'Not my grass, anyhow, and I'll never use it. My sheep stay in the pasture. Look, Bud, I'd go up and help you, but I'm busy myself. Serving papers. Court in Cibola next month.'

'I heard about them papers,' said Bud, laughing. 'Heard that your mileage was costing the county a-plenty. Ninety consecutive miles to Cibola, they said, and every mile a mint.'

Anson Hunter lifted up his head and gazed at Cremony with innocent eyes. 'They used to work that mileage stuff up north,' he said. 'In Idaho.' A hell of hot hate flamed in Bat Cremony's eyes. He fought it back, but two had seen; John and Bud. 'One sheriff was stirring up all sorts of trouble, so he could get plenty of mileage, making arrests and serving subpœnas. He was drawing down twice the salary the sheriff of London was getting. So they cut out the mileage in Idaho, and put their sheriffs on a salary.'

'Well, I've got to move on,' said Cremony. 'Good luck, Bud. They're planning to give you a building bee, you know. I'll be there, or send someone to represent. If you need anything from Catorce, go get it. By-by. Watch your behavior.'

He rode away. Hunter rose up then. 'I'll be going, too. Won't you gentlemen come to the hotel and have dinner — supper, I mean — with me?'

Bud chuckled. 'That's dead against our principles. Hotels are for strangers. When La Huerta comes visiting us, we feed 'em. When we come visiting, La Huerta feeds us. Them's the rules. Thanks, and all that. But I've never taken a meal in Pappy's hotel yet, and I don't aim to begin now.'

Hunter laughed. 'See you later, then. I want to hear some more of your stories. Interesting, if true.'

'True, my foot!' said Marble. 'We see to

it that they're interesting, whether or no. We make a point of it.'

'I can well believe as much,' said Hunter gaily. 'Good night, gentlemen.'

He went his way then. John's eyes met Bud's. 'That jigger!' said Bud, barely above a whisper. 'In this up to his neck... Did you see Cremony's eyes?'

'Did I? "In Idaho," says Hunter, and made his eyes round. Baby stare. Sneer in his voice and curling lip. Blackmail. Cremony will kill him.'

'I thought Bat was going to shoot, just now,' said Bud. 'Say, John — I'm not so keen about letting my gun hang on a peg, Corby or no Corby. Running around half-dressed — it ain't hardly decent.'

'Keep your voice down,' said John. He glanced back through the open door. 'Nobody near, but we can't be too careful. Fowler, Bat Cremony, and this Hunter person! How could Hunter know your house was burned unless he was part and parcel of the plan? Maybe he planned it. He seems to hold the whip hand over Cremony.

"*Idaho*," says he, and Cremony went off like blasting powder in a backlog... I'm chilly, myself, without my gun.' John held his head between his hands. 'Oh, mamma! Hunter doesn't know a cow from a curling-iron. How does he come in? What does he want of your ranch?'

'Well I know. And you are to consider these words as hissed,' said Bud. 'Hissed in your ear, like the book says. Hunter was with this railroad that we pray about. Surveyor. First survey... Let me think. What with?... Guess, then... Got it! Got it, by golly! Water is what Hunter wants. Olvidado water. Soft water. Hunter and Fowler and Bat. Wynken — and Blynken — and Nod! John, this is a bad water country. John, that railroad was never built. Never built, because that railroad found no good water. These three misbegotten dogs ——' Bud gulped. 'I didn't mean that. I beg pardon from all dogs. These three want Olvidado water to sell to that railroad!'

'You lift that mortgage tomorrow morning,' said John.

'I will not. Yank was all wrong about where to hang our guns, but Yank was dead right about evidence. We know the whole story, but we can't prove one word of it. No court would hold any of them five minutes for what we can prove. That mortgage rides. They'll make another clever play and this time we'll take them in the act.'

'I get you, Bud. If you pay up, everything stops. Right you are. Looky, yonder, Bud. See what's coming? Your friends have heard the news and they're coming to condole.'

'I see where we get some supper,' said Bud. 'But we'll get our guns first.'

Condolers came, condoling. As prophesied, they carried Bud and John away to supper. Afterward, they all came back to the saloon together, for a few drinks, a few songs, a few stories. Also, fresh condolers appearing, old and new joined in a long, long condoling, a strong, strong condoling and a condolence altogether. Perhaps there were a few more drinks. Between nine and ten, old Eusebio appeared on the scene, quiet, unassuming, modestly in the background.

After Eusebio's drink — not before — he caught Bud's eye. When opportunity served, he pressed a scrap of paper into Bud's hand. Bud slipped that scrap of paper into a pocket, and moved away. Eusebio slipped through the door. Bud took the note from his pocket then, and read it.

We found your steers. Come home, if you can find the way. But if you wake us up when you come, you'll never see your steers again.

GEORGE

CHAPTER XV

'IT WAS my idea, entirely,' said George complacently. 'I mistrusted where the cows might be, all along. Can't imagine who told Cremony about that place, for few are left to know, who played with me on Fiddler's Green just twenty years ago.'

Shane rolled a slow eye at Sam. The four friends sat at a late breakfast in George Walker's pleasant kitchen. Doors and windows were wide open, and the high sun peered over the treetops.

'When I used to operate there,' said George dreamily, 'I thought it was a tough lay. Now, looking back, I can see that I was having the time of my young life. You leave them cattle there, Bud. After-while, when you're not so crowded, you might lead a committee down there and show them. Even a jury might suspect something, evidence or no evidence.'

'Was that the only way in?' John Marble asked the question. Behind John's back, Sam shook his head slightly.

'Oh, no,' said George glibly. 'Another trail on the west side. Handy layout, that was.' George did not propose to have any delving into Sam Clark's past.

As for Sam himself, he now wore every appearance of a sheepish citizen; but Shane's face was all one warm and golden smile. He stacked his dishes; he filled the tea-kettle, and built the fire anew.

'Well, Bud,' said Shane, 'you have all the dope, now. Hunter tipped his hand to you. You know exactly what has happened, and why. What are you going to do about it? Just as you say, we can't fasten any single act to any one man. We now have one definite fact. Hunter knew, without being told, that your house had gone up in smoke. That's all. Cow-stealing or arson — if we try to get a warrant for any one man, and all we get is a horse-laugh.'

'Hunter is the weak link,' said Bud. 'The play is to work on Hunter. He said he was going up to the mill and I told him I was going up there today. We'll rig up a deadfall for him.'

'Do that. You do it — you and John. I am an industrious man,' said Shane, 'and I long for a scamper after the cattle. But George and Sam and I, we are supposed to be far, far away. It would never do for us to be seen here. Fowler and Bat would be on their guard at once. Deeply as I regret it, duty compels us three to stay here and sleep all day, while you two take a horse-ride.'

Bud and John avoided the business section, following byways. Above the town they came to the main road. The narrow valley of the Borachón is richest alluvial soil, and every square foot of it, as far as possible, is saved for farmland. Buildings and yards cling to the hillsides, twisting ditches are carved from the hillsides, twisting roads clamber on the hillsides, crossing over and back and back again to avoid the loopings of that shining river. A green and pleasant valley, and those low-walled homes were pleasant there behind the sheltering hills.

Inquiry was made of brown farmers. Oh, yes. The Señor Hunter had passed by. He was riding that Butterfly horse of Señor Fowler's — that *palomilla*. Veree slow he rides. How far ahead? An hour, perhaps. Less, perhaps. *Quien sabe?*

The two cowmen pushed on briskly. Twelve miles above town, the valley splits to three forks. Dark and steep, the narrow canyon of Walnut Creek comes down from the south. Borachón proper, the main stream, is the middle fork; the mill road follows that. Half a mile above the mouth of Walnut, the low, dry valley of the Carrizo winds in from the north. And where Carrizo joined the Borachón, they met Dan Corby, riding down the Carrizo on a brisk trot.

'I was coming to town to join your happy party,' said Corby. 'Listen, I saw something funny just now. Who is it that rides a big white horse — big horse, sixteen hands high, long, wide, and handsome?'

'That's our man Cremony,' said John. 'He's our deputy sheriff, you know, and he's out on business, calling 'em in to come to court. Why?'

'Well, he came down the main valley, just

now. And there was another guy below, coming this way, riding a cream-colored pony. He got just one look at the white horse, and he turned off into the timber, instanter, and hid there. That interested me, so I rode behind a tree and watched. The man with the white horse quit the main valley and rode up the little canyon that branches off, just below here. The man on the cream-colored horse took a good long wait for himself. Then he came back and went up the main road. What's the answer? Is that fellow on the dodge?'

'That was Hunter,' said Bud happily. 'Hunter, and he's afraid of Cremony, out of town. That's fine. Come on, we've got to overtake Hunter before he gets to the mill. Lots of news for you, Dan, good news. No time to tell you now. Our business is with Hunter. You and John take him with you, back to John's place. When you get there, John will tell you the news, up to date. Then you two can take Hunter to pieces and see what makes him tick. We've got to hurry... Let me talk to Hunter. I've got it all doped out. You two play up. You're going to take Hunter for a bear hunt. Come on, let's lope!'

They overtook Hunter, halfway to the mill. Bud greeted him gaily.

'Here's your chance, young man. You're playing in luck. This is Dan Corby, Mr. Hunter. We met him at the forks of the creek, just below here. He was coming to town from John's ranch, and he tells us he saw three brown bears this morning at daylight. We heard you was on the road ahead of us. So I told Dan about you, and how you wanted a bear.'

'You'll never get a better chance,' said Marble. 'Tom Spence, down the creek, he's got a couple of good hounds, trained hounds. I'll send my boy Bill for Tom and his hounds. Bright and early, tomorrow, we'll take the trail. You can get a deer, afterward, any time.'

Hunter hesitated perceptibly. 'This is kind of you, gentlemen. I'd like to go, of course. But there are difficulties. The fact is, I'm not used to riding and I'm tired out already.'

'Shucks, we can fix that,' said Bud eagerly. 'That horse you're riding is rough-gaited. No wonder you're tired. I'm surprised at Fowler for fitting you out with a horse like that. I am so. And that saddle is no good, either. You take my horse and saddle. This plug of mine is a pacer. Easy as a rocking-chair. We'll let my stirrups out to fit you, and you'll be fine as silk. Farther than it is to the mill, of course, but you can't afford to miss this chance. Bears are scarce. I'm going up to the mill, anyhow — like I told you, yesterday. I'll tell Price about you and take your horse back to Fowler, and tell him to look for you when he sees you coming.'

'That's fine for me,' said Hunter doubt-fully. 'But how about you? How will you get home?'

Bud laughed. 'Why, this is my country,' he said. 'Anybody in La Huerta will let me have a horse and saddle. Or I can borrow a saddle and ride my load of lumber home. Going to hire a man to haul it for me, and I'll have to go with him, anyhow, to show him the way. Wagon-road goes all around Robin

Hood's barn to get to my place. Don't
you worry about me. You go and get that
bear.'

So Hunter gave thanks and went. After
the stirrups were adjusted, Bud rode mill-
wards up the Borachón. The others turned
back and followed the Carrizo trail. It was
a long trail, an up-and-down trail, a trail
that swept gigantically across the dizzy
steeps of Star Mountain. But Anson Hunter
was in no shape to appreciate that tremen-
dous outlook. He was a weary man when
they reached ONO, and gladly accepted
Marble's invitation to sleep until supper-
time.

It was a good supper and Hunter felt better
after a steaming cup of coffee. No boy Bill
was in evidence. Hunter noticed that, but
assumed that the boy Bill had gone to bring
the hounds.

Supper over, they drew their chairs together before a blazing fire. John brought
forth a fiddle. He played a merry tune. A
wistful tune next, and then a sad one. He
put the fiddle by, he tapped out his pipe upon

the hearthstone, filled it afresh, lit up and
leaned over to address his guest. His voice
was gentle, with a rising note.

'Why are you afraid of Cremony?' said
John Marble.

Hunter jerked in his chair. Dan Corby's
hand touched his elbow.

'What was it that Cremony did in Idaho?'
said Dan.

Hunter's lips were dry. His throat closed
together, sand crawled beneath his eyelids,
and John Marble's gentle voice was dreadful
in his ear.

'Why did Fowler have Bud's house burned
down?'

Bud did not go to the mill. He waited
around the next bend for a short hour. He
fired two shots then. Riding down the canyon, he passed the Carrizo and came to the
mouth of Walnut. There, close beside the
trail Cremony had taken, he tossed his two
empty cartridge shells. He went on down
the road to La Huerta. Two miles farther
on, where the road made a sheltered elbow

on a hillside, he dismounted where stony ground would leave no boot-tracks.

He tied the saddle rope around Butterfly's neck and took the bridle from Butterfly's head. The leather was old and dry and cracked. Tying the end of one rein around a cedar bough, Bud took a half-hitch around his hand and surged back, breaking the rein midway. He then performed the like service for the other rein. He put the bridle back on Butterfly's head, he coiled the rope on Butterfly's saddle, turned Butterfly's head toward the mill again, and gave Butterfly a vigorous start with a brushwood stick across his rump. Butterfly went flying up the Borachón road.

Bud untied the broken pieces of bridle rein and carried them with him. He clambered down the hill, letting no foot fall until it touched upon a stone. He had chosen the spot for his latest exploit because, just below him, but out of sight, Sabedeo Serrano's little house clung to the hillside, in a sheltered dimple, close above his fields. Sabedeo was a bachelor, and one who owed Bud love and service, for service rendered long ago, in an hour of great need.

Sabedeo was at home and did according to Bud's desires, with no questioning. He hitched two yellow mules to a dish-wheeled wagon, and went creaking down the road to La Huerta. A roll of bedding was in that wagon, alfalfa hay for the night's feed for the yellow mules, and a loose tarpaulin. Bud Copeland lay upon the hay, covered by the tarpaulin. At dark, Sabedeo delivered Bud safely at George Walker's place, and then drove back uptown for his slender shopping.

At eight o'clock, a whisper rose in La Huerta. A riderless horse had been found on the Borachón; a saddled horse, a bridle with broken reins. The whisper became a buzzing. It was a horse of Jake Fowler's, that Butterfly horse of his. Young Hunter had ridden that horse — the stranger at the hotel. He had started for the mill. Borachón farmers were searching the hills. The buzzing became a tumult. Lige King had just driven down from the mill. Hunter had not reached the mill and no man had seen him since early morning. Had there been foul play? Murder? This is business for the sheriff. Where is Bat Cremony?

The deputy sheriff reached town at ten. He had served a summons at the head of Walnut, coming back over the hills by Kennedy's. No supper; Kennedy not at home. Too late for a search tonight. Everybody out at daylight tomorrow, said the deputy.

Cremony did not sleep well that night.

CHAPTER XVI

THE deputy had named daylight for the gathering, but he had been all too hopeful. Daylight found a scanty ten at the wagon-yard. Recruits dribbled in at intervals, two or three at a time. The doors of the Oasis Saloon were opened wide and much used. Sunrise was near when Cremony announced that he was ready to start. Something like fifty horsemen, Mexicans and Americans, were waiting. Cremony turned white Jumbo to face the crowd, and held up his hand.

'Friends, we don't know whether this man has been killed or not. It looks bad, of course. There was no reason why he should have left the main road. A cowman might have been off over the hills, anywhere, chasing cattle. When a cowman's horse comes in, the first thought is that he has had a fall, and is waiting somewhere with a broken leg. But this man Hunter was no cowman.'

'That isn't all,' said Jake Fowler. 'You all know that old horse I let Hunter have — old

Butterfly. He can't go fast enough to fall down, so we can put aside any theory of accident — that kind of accident.' Fowler was afoot, having come to guide and not to ride. He looked up at Cremony, and malice was in his eyes. Privately, Fowler was not ill-pleased, remembering Hunter's promise of what would happen in case of accidents. 'He seemed to have plenty of money,' Fowler added. 'Someone may have noticed that.'

'If he was killed,' said Cremony, 'we don't know where he was killed, or what became of the body.' His brow furrowed with anxious effort. 'The body may be where he was killed, or it may have been carried off and hidden. It may have been thrown into the river. Aguilar, you pick yourself four or five men, and follow the river up. Search all the fields and find out all they know at every farm. The rest of us will go up to Joe García's — where the horse was found, and scatter out. There's a big country to search. Fowler, when you get another bunch of men together, send 'em up after us. One thing more. If anyone finds Hunter — or his body — he wants to ride up on a hill and build a fire and whoever sees it is to build another fire, and so on, to call everybody back. Otherwise, we are liable to hunt all day for nothing. Let's go.'

'Hold on, Bat!' Tom Powers, the blacksmith, rode up a few steps and spoke earnestly. 'You're forgetting something. You want to have a lot of searching done right here in town. If young Hunter was murdered, what could be easier than to put him in a wagon and slip down in the night and dump the corpse in somebody's field? You don't want to miss a bet like that.'

'You're right, Powers,' said the deputy. 'You and Fowler organize another posse, then, and search out the town. Send a couple of good men to ride a circle below town, to see if there are any fresh tracks leading out to the desert. If a dead man was buried out there in the middle of the sand-dunes, he might be found in fifty years, or never.'

'I'm going with you,' said the blacksmith. 'Let the old men organize the posse — there's plenty of them. What's the matter with your little old justice of the peace? Let him help Fowler run the town, him and our lawyers. You lead on, Mister Deputy, and I'll be right at your stirrup.'

Organization of the home guard posse was well under way when Bud Copeland pushed through the crowd and spoke to Fowler.

'What's all this?' said Bud. 'We just heard that someone had been killed. Who was it?'

'Someone missing, at least. Possibly killed. We don't know. That man Hunter. You know him.'

'Hunter? That young fellow from the East?' Bud's eyes widened. 'Why, who'd want to kill him?'

'We don't know what has happened yet,' said Fowler. 'His horse was found near the García farm. That's all we know, so far.'

'Well, why didn't you let us know?' said Bud. 'We think we're plenty good enough to go along in any company. Just by chance that we heard something was not just right, somewheres.'

'Let who know?' said Fowler, reasonably enough. 'We thought you went home yesterday.' Then his eye took notice of the horse Bud was riding. 'Oh, I see! You're down at George Walker's. That's old Eusebio's horse.'

'It is not. This is my horse. Traded horses and saddles with Eusebio, yesterday. Well, I'll be jogging. We haven't had breakfast yet. George came home, late last night — him and Easy McFarland and that lisping jasper of mine. Them three and me — there's four for you!' said Bud. His eyes lit with enthusiasm and he patted his own chest approvingly. 'When we overtake Cremony's posse, it will be something worth while!'

'Take Eusebio with you,' said Fowler. 'That old man is an A Number One tracker.'

'Eusebio's sick-a-bed,' said Bud, and turned to go. But he paused to speak in an undertone to Sabedeo, who was putting the harness on the yellow mules.

'Zebedee,' said Bud, 'I sure overlooked a

bet last night. Careless of me. Going up, yesterday, I asked Pascual and Jacinto if they had seen young Hunter. You drop in to Pascual's and tell them to be sure to remember to forget that they saw me. I should have had you tell them last night.'

Sabadeo looked up with a troubled face. 'But eef I am too late? Eef they have told already? Weel that not be bad for you? Get me a horse and a gun, Señor Bud, and I weel ride weeth you, all the way.'

Bud laughed and clapped his hand on Sabedeo's shoulder. 'You're a faithful old cuss, Zebedee, ain't you? Don't you fret about me. Somehow, I don't think Pascual and Jacinto will give me away. Shocking bad memories, both of 'em. Besides, they'll be riding the hills, likely, looking for the corpse. Don't you worry, *amigo*. There ain't no corpse. I know where Hunter is, and no hair of his head is hurt. Keep it quiet. This is a private magic of my own — *una brujería, sabe?*'

That anxious brown face cleared. 'But how are you the devil!' said loyal Sabedeo.

Borachón farmers swelled the posse;
lumber-jacks, mill men, reinforcements from
La Huerta, men from Walnut Creek. Men
rode on every ridge of all the cedared ridges
of the great triangle that was drained by the
Borachón. Men rode in every canyon and
draw. Men rode the wide pineland country
between the mill and the summit.

Harry Moore and Strap Harrison led a
bunch to comb the Rinconada, sending one
man by a short-cut trail to bear the news to
Dorayme. On a similar errand, Ed Little
went on from the head of Walnut, following
the ridge to Los Genios; and the mill-boss
had dispatched a rider across the divide to
warn the Indian Agency and the eastern
slope. Lant Stewart and Clovis Lujan,
with four others, rode the tangled maze
of the Carrizo, twisting draws and hidden
meadows and pinewood ridge, everyone the
same.

Orders were to hold all strangers. But there
were no strangers. Nothing had been heard
of the missing man, no trace of him was
found; no fire flamed from any hill. True,

one sinister discovery had been made. Just where the Walnut Creek trail turned up from the Borachón, Ed Little had found two empty cartridge-shells, forty-fives, freshly fired, still smelling of burnt powder. This might mean nothing. Forty-five caliber revolvers were common. More of them than the sum total of all other guns. Or — it might mean a great deal. Henry Hall brought this news to Cremony, overtaking him above the mill where he rode with the dwindling vanguard of the posse.

Men whispered together apart, in knots and clusters. It was Len Strong, the yard-master, who spoke aloud.

'Bat, you left the mill about ten in the morning, you say? And then went up Walnut Creek, serving papers?'

A red spot showed upon Cremony's cheek. 'I certainly did. I had subpœnas for the Jones boys as witnesses in a cow-stealing case on the Reservation. If you mean to ask me if I killed young Hunter, I'm here to tell you that I didn't. It might have been me, of course. I was up here, and Hunter had started this way. I could see this coming, hours ago. It was just a matter of time until someone began to think of me as a possibility. That's all right with me. Natural enough. It might have been any of us. To all practical purposes, every man on the posse, first and last, is under suspicion, me with the rest. If any of you think that I'm the murderer, I'm willing to give up my guns and go back to town under guard, wearing my own handcuffs. On one condition. That is, that you keep up the search.'

'Forget it!' said Roy Johnson. He was a ranchman from Walnut Creek. 'I was riding the hills alone, all day yesterday, and I didn't see a soul. Bat said a mouthful. Until we find this stranger alive, or pin the job on the right man if Hunter has really been murdered, every mother's son of us is under suspicion, unless he can prove where he was. For all we know, this man Hunter may have gone batty. That happens. We may find him counting his fingers, with berries in his hair. You've got no more on Bat than you have on me. Don't act

like a pack of wild jackasses.   Bat isn't
going to run away.   He's got too much
stuff to leave behind.'

Bat was not so sure of that, stuff or no stuff.
No man rode with him now, but fear rode
with him, fear and frantic hate.   He remembered, all too well, what Hunter had said —
sneering, insolent devil!   In case of Hunter's
death, a letter would be mailed to Idaho.
That was no bluff — and when he said Idaho,
that was no figure of speech or algebraic x.
Cremony knew what threatened him in
Idaho.   A noose.   Murder, brutal and cow-
ardly, proved to the hilt.   What a drunken
fool he had been!

A black thought came to his mind.   Fowler?   What if Fowler had contrived to have
Hunter murdered, ridding himself of two unwelcome partners at one stroke, keeping the
rich pickings of Olvidado for himself, unshared?   Sweat started down his face, his
heart pounded at his ribs.   He drew rein and
turned, trembling with hate, half-minded to
ride straight to town, to cut short all Fowler's

triumph with a bullet through that scheming head.

Craziness! Fowler might plan it, but he can't risk it. He isn't in touch with anyone he can trust — anyone but me. He spoke aloud, hoarsely. His throat was parched, his brain on fire. 'That was how I got started, as middleman. What am I — a white-livered fool? Ten to one, Hunter is alive this minute. Damn him, he may be doing this to torture me. To scare me into running away, maybe. What if he is working with Fowler? To scare me out, to share that railroad money, half-and-half.' He rode back toward the mill for half a hundred yards; he turned again and set his face to the north, riding slowly.

Noon was high above him. He rode in Cat's Cradle, the last high meadow where a hump of divide was wide and flat, making a high tableland between a deep pass on the south and a high pass on the north. Low ridges hemmed that meadow roundabout, making it a walled amphitheater, a mile long. Low notches broke away on every side; east to Clear Creek, south to the mill, west to the

Carrizo, north to the plunging trail that fell away into the deeps of Cedar Creek. This was a natural cross-roads, but there had been no fresh tracks on any trail. One by one the posse had turned aside, each to follow up a winding draw. The blacksmith had been the last to go. Cremony had sent the blacksmith across into the head of Clear Creek.

The north opened out before him. Panic fear urged him to flight, to ply whip and spur. He reined Jumbo to a halt, and fought desperately to regain self-control. If he could choose to abandon all his gains, with one night's hard riding he could be beyond pursuit. Riding northeast, he could go four hundred miles before he came to a railroad track, four hundred miles before he would see a telegraph pole, once he was past the Government line to Fort Stanton, a dozen miles ahead. *Coward!* And lose Catorce, lose his farms, the Oasis, lose all the heaped-up gold in the El Paso banks? Impossible. Yet if he went back, if he should be held on suspicion of Hunter's death? If a sheriff came from Idaho? Cremony shuddered. Ruin to go on.

Ruin to turn back. If he knew that Hunter was dead ——

A horseman rode on the western ridge and stood there, outlined against the sky. George Walker. He held a rifle before him, crosswise on the saddle.

Cremony looked back over his shoulder. The blacksmith was just riding into the meadow from the Clear Creek Gap. Flight, then. A hundred yards would reach cover. Would a rifle bullet find him first? That flight was never started. He reined Jumbo to a slow walk. Fear clutched his heart. From the pines on the northern ridges, Bud Copeland rode slowly into the little clearing of the Cedar Creek Gap. Shane McFarland followed; then Sam Clark. They rode slowly to meet him.

An arrest? No good to resist. Have to brazen it out. Cremony forced himself to speak, in a high, strained voice. 'Hello, Bud! You fellows find anything? Any news?'

Bud rode at ease, loose-reined, both hands on the saddle-horn, 'No news,' he said cheerfully. 'Nothing particular, anyway. I heard

that someone was holding Strap Harrison
under guard, but I don't know if there's a
word of truth in that or not.' He shrugged
his shoulders. 'When we get all worked up
and excited, you can hear most anything.'
Bud looked down at his booted foot and
slapped idly at his leg with the loose end of
a bridle rein.

Blood flooded back into Cremony's face.
'Strap Harrison? For killing Hunter?'

Bud looked up, surprised. 'Oh, no! Nothing like that. Stealing cattle, they said —
him and some other fellows. Nothing important. Killing Hunter? Shucks, no! Everybody
seems to think you killed Hunter, yourself.'

'Before God, Bud, I didn't do it! I haven't
seen Hunter since night before last.'

'So he was telling us,' said Bud pleasantly.
'Bat, I'm afraid this is your finish with that
deputy sheriff job. Hunter went visiting with
John Marble, it seems. So you lost your head
and raised a hullabaloo all over the shop.
Folks will never quit laughing about this.'

'I don't give a damn,' said Cremony. 'I
sure thought that man had been murdered.'

George and the blacksmith joined the party here.

'Hunter is waiting for us at the head of Carrizo,' said Bud. 'Him and John Marble and a friend of John's. Somebody saw you here, Bat, and we judged we'd better come over and head you off before you rode yourself to death.' Bud held the reins in his crippled right hand now. His left hand dropped to his side, near to where his loosely belted gun swung low against his thigh.

'All right, laugh your fool heads off,' said Cremony, mopping at his sweat-stained face. 'I'm getting more out of this than any of you fellows. Just as you said, everyone seemed to think that I had killed Hunter. Why, the blacksmith here — I sent him down Clear Creek, and he turned right back to watch me, afraid I was going to skip the country.'

'That's right,' laughed the blacksmith. 'I'm not sure yet but what that was just what you was meaning to do, when it comes to cases. You were one scared man, right from the first. I had my eye on you.'

'Well, let's drag it,' said Cremony.

'One thing more, before we go,' said Bud. 'Cremony...why did you kill my dog?'

Cremony streaked for his gun. Bud was quicker. A bullet crashed into Cremony's shoulder just as his gun cleared the holster. He dropped the gun, howling.

'Hop down, Bat, and let's see did I kill you,' said Bud. 'I could have done that, of course, but I didn't want to let you off so easy. You got a lot to answer for.'

Shane kicked the fallen gun aside and helped Cremony, half-falling, half-crawling, from his horse. Whirling terrors of the day had been too much for outraged nerves, and the wings of death had brushed him as they passed; the man was broken. Desperate, abject, his dry lips faltered in a frantic babbling.

'Jake Fowler was in this, all the way,' said Cremony. 'Damn him, he goes down with me.'

'Oh, we know all that,' said Bud wearily. 'You can't turn State's evidence. Hunter beat you to it. He opened up his heart. You tell your story to the judge — you and Jake... How about it, Shane? Is he going to croak on us?'

'He's all right,' Shane reported. 'May lose an arm or two, but he'll live to stretch hemp yet. Plug him up with a piece of shirt-tail, and he'll make out, fine.'

'Take him down to the mill, the best way you can,' said Bud to the blacksmith. 'Sam can go with you, as far as the mill or till you meet up with some of your posse. Cremony might fall off, and he's too heavy for one man to lift back on. Sam, as soon as you get shut of Cremony, you'd better lope up and over- take us. We'll pick up John and Dan Corby and Hunter and beat it down the Carrizo to town. I'm going to give a little party down- town — quite infernal. Powers, you stay right with Cremony. He's under arrest. Stealin' cattle and one thing and another. You hang on to him. Let me have them hand- cuffs of Bat's, will you? And I wish you'd try to hold your posse back awhile, so I can have an hour or two head start on them. I don't want 'em boiling in to spoil my surprise. If you think our deputy can stand the trip, bring him down in a buggy. If he is too sick, you stay there and nurse him along. Take good care of him!'

CHAPTER XVII

No FRESH tracks leading down to the desert — no shod tracks. If any dead man rode that way, he had used a barefooted horse for his flight. No fresh wagon-tracks leading down to the desert, unless it were on the main road. And it was sure that no dead man had driven down the main road, because three wagons, coming late to the desert edge, had camped together beside the road where they came to the first pool of Borachón water, and no wagon had passed that camp during the night. No dead man ghastly in any field of all La Huerta's fields; every nook and corner was well searched within the first four hours of daylight. After which the able-bodied rode hot-foot up the Borachón to help there in the criss-cross mountains and tangled woods. The town was left to women and children and old men.

Jake Fowler was not an old man, but he did not go; nor Frank Pickett, the town's young lawyer; nor the clerks in Fowler's

store. It is to the unprosperous that we turn
in trouble. Little is expected from the thrifty;
a circumstance which is no hindrance to added
thriving.

The young doctor had gone with the first.
But the shaggy Scotch doctor was old, the
justice of the peace was old, and Pappy Wil-
son of the Garden House was old and bent.
These three sat on the porch of the Garden
House. Ellis Fletcher, leaning heavily on his
cane, came late and limping to make four;
the town's old lawyer, long retired. Father
Duran joined them to make five. The mur-
mur of bees was drowsy in the empty streets,
and they told sad stories of sorrows past.
Twice before, twice in as many decades, there
had been a man missing in this little town;
twice a broken body had been found to speak
of murder done; crimes brought home to no
man. Curious, said the old men, thin-voiced
and quietly; all these years we have sat by
some fire which was a murderer's, laughed
at his whimsies, and clasped his hand and
bade him God-speed! — Why, it may have
been one of us, said the shaggy doctor.

The wagon-yard was empty, the little Mexican stores were closed, the barber shop was closed, the blacksmith's fire was cold. Morning dragged on to noon, and no word came down from hill or mill or the farmlands of the Borachón. Noon brought high laughter of racing children, shrill shoutings from the playgrounds of the school. The bell was startling that called an end to play, and silence fell again in the green, sleepy streets.

Jake Fowler sat alone in his pleasant private office. He sorted papers on his desk, some to docket and file away, some dropped into a waste-basket, some laid aside for leisured consideration at another time. He did not feel in the mood for any heavy concentration now; his thoughts were far away. He paused in his labors, often and long, to look out through open window and open door to that small, pleasant yard of his; he drummed lightly on the desk with soft fingers, or sat motionless, with unseeing eyes, reflecting, smiling, reviewing past and plans.

Young Pickett had dropped in for a while,

taking instructions as to certain timber lands. Pickett was by way of being jackal to this lion. Had any word come down from the search party? Nothing yet.

After the lawyer's departure, Fowler smiled again; almost broadly. Here was a great piece of luck! — If Hunter was dead, that is. Bat had never killed Hunter. Hunter had Bat cowed — no doubt about that. Had Bat right under his thumb, and Bat took that threat about Idaho at face value. That had been a shrewd touch of Hunter's, to point out that he was taking no precaution to insure safety, other than that letter which was to be mailed in case of accident. Convincing, that was. Clever fellow, Hunter. And Bat believed him, all right... Bat would have to leave. Bat would never dare to stay. That was murder surely, in Idaho, or wherever the place was which Hunter knew, and Bat Cremony knew. Hunter dead, Cremony a fugitive, with death the forfeit for return! Fine! I will have that railroad money, all of it, unshared. For the first time, I can start to work in a big way. I will pull down my

barns—— Fowler frowned and put an unwelcome thought away. He leaned back in
his chair.

Stuff and nonsense! Day-dreams. Hunter
wasn't dead, of course. Who would kill him?
And why? Bat wouldn't dare to, under the
circumstances. Bat would be the last man on
earth. Hunter wasn't dead. Drunk, probably. That's it, for a dollar! All respecta-
bility in town, saving his face. Gone up in the
hills for a solitary bout of whiskey swilling,
overdid it and let his horse get away. — Or,
made acquaintance with someone up there.
It may have been a hold-over acquaintance,
for all I know. Someone he knew when he
was here before. Some old toper. Kindred
spirit. Lot of soaks up the creek.

Again the sound of young laughter in the
street, and merry voices high and chattering;
school was out. Fowler frowned at this interruption. When that gay boistering ceased,
he took up his anxious thoughts again... That
would be tough. Pretty hard, after seeing the
certainty of fingering all that Olvidado
money, to have to cut it three ways, after all.

Wonder how much I can screw out of the railroad company? They might go high... That Hunter! Something might happen to him yet — another time. If I knew anyone I could trust. — For the second time, Fowler checked his thought that he might not betray it to himself.

A rhymed and throbbing beat of spurs in a merry jingle, a shadow against the sun; Bud Copeland came along the path to that open door. His walk was a jaunty swagger, his lips tucked in a smile.

Fowler sprang up and a splotch of color came to his cheek. 'Did you find Hunter? Was he killed, or hurt?'

'Nothing like that. Your questions are a little mixed, you know. Hard to answer, yes or no.' The smile grew broader. 'They're chasing around up there, looking for him. Plenty without me, so I sort of oozed away, and sidled on back. Plenty without Bud, and I had a little business to 'tend to.'

Fowler waved him to a chair. Bud pushed his hat well back, rolled a cigarette, savored a puff or two, crossed his knees and leaned

back in his chair, hands clasped behind his
neck. 'Yes, I thought I might as well lift
that mortgage, so ——'

'You — what?' said Fowler sharply.
His face was a study of incredulity and
dismay.

'Lift my mortgage. Gosh, Mr. Fowler, I
don't want to lose that ranch. My father
was the first man who ever lived there since
the world began. Sometimes,' said Bud
dreamily, 'sometimes I think I'd like to get
it fixed up — if it could be managed — so
that place couldn't be sold away from my
name and blood. So if my grandchildren
went out in the world and got their wings
scorched, they could always come back to
the old place and scratch out a living there...
I haven't named them yet. Want to pick out
some real good names. It's a damn' shame the
names they gyp off on some of the kids when
they're too little to protect themselves...
Where was I? Oh, yes, I know. So, me not
knowing anything about the legal formalities
about releasing a mortgage, and maybe having the release recorded and so on and so

forth, world without end, why, I stopped at Ellis Fletcher's, and washed off some of the sweat and dust, and asked Ellis to come down here as lookout for me.'

Fowler made no reply. He was touched in the quick place of his heart. Disappointed greed and baffled cunning twisted his smooth face to an evil mask; or, more truly, the smooth mask fell away, leaving the evil bare for any eye to see.

'Ellis isn't as spry as he used to be, but he's peggin' on down,' said Bud. 'Pickett being your lawyer and all, I judged it would be best for me to get Ellis. You may want to have Pickett in yourself. We want to get this fixed up all shipshape and legal. Here's Ellis now, and Pickett tagging along. Ellis told him what was up, I reckon.'

The old lawyer and the young one came to the door together. 'Mr. Fowler, I have taken the liberty of asking Mr. Pickett to come with me,' said Fletcher stiffly. 'In any case, we would have been obliged to procure from him the necessary forms. As you know, I have done no legal business for years. I came here today only to oblige the son of an old and dear friend.'

'You dig up the mortgage, Mr. Fowler,' said Bud. 'Here's my part.' He tossed Dan Corby's check on the desk. 'Fifty-six hundred dollars. Rebate coming to me on the interest, you know. Let the lawyers figure that out and then you can pay me the difference.'

Fowler held the check between extended hands; hands which trembled a little. 'Daniel J. Corby.' He read the name harshly. 'Never heard of him. How do I know that this check is good?'

'You don't,' said Bud. 'Turn it over and read the endorsements. Shane, and John Marble, and me. You know us. And they're all over at the saloon now, if you want to verify the signatures.'

'But, after all, a check is not money,' said Fowler. 'This check is not legal tender.'

'You take a singular position, sir,' said Ellis Fletcher dryly. 'One would almost suppose that you did not want this mortgage paid. For a man of your experience, you surprise me. This situation is as old as law. The procedure is familiar and simple. Mr. Pickett and myself will fill out the prescribed forms. After those papers are signed, we will send them by registered mail to be held in escrow by the Cibola Bank. When the check has been paid, the bank will then have the release properly recorded. The transaction will be then complete.'

'That is correct, Mr. Fowler,' said Pickett. 'That is the customary procedure, safeguarding all parties.'

The older lawyer bowed acknowledgment. 'If you will oblige us, then, by bringing the indicated forms from your office?'

Pickett departed. Bud went with him as far as the door of the Oasis Saloon. Beyond that door he found his friends, together with the unhappy Hunter, a haggard and collapsed figure of a man, stunned and bewildered by the failure of his golden hopes and the danger heavy over his head. To bear him company, Gradual George remained, together with Sam Clark, that joyful citizen and true man by brevet; while Bud returned to his legal perplexities with three friends in tow —

Corby and Shane and John; to verify their signatures upon the Corby check, and to be witnesses to the next transfer of that check and to the purpose of that transfer.

Those wearisome papers were signed at last. Shane and Pickett departed together as a joint commission, delegated to post those papers by registered mail. John and Dan Corby followed; and Ellis Fletcher reached for his cane.

'Can you spare me a minute yet, Mr. Fletcher?' said Bud. 'There are two questions that I would like to ask you before you go. As you know, there will be a little more than a hundred and twenty-five dollars coming to me from Friend Fowler, when that check is paid. Would you be willing to accept that hundred and twenty-five, more or less, as a retainer, so I could depend upon you to look after my interests for me? — No, don't give me your answer now. Sleep on it, and tell me tomorrow. You see, the Bee Line is going to buy the Olvidado water from me ——'

A groan that was half a sob burst from

Fowler's lips, for that lost fortune which his hand had touched. Bud turned a bright face Fowler's way, and shook a reproving finger at him. 'Naughty, naughty!' said Bud. 'Papa spank!' Then he turned to the lawyer again. 'The railroad wants soft water for their engines, and Olvidado is all the soft water there is. Well and good. But I want to keep enough water for ranch purposes. That calls for safeguards and many a whereas and aforesaid, and I hope you can see it through for me.'

'I think I know now what my answer will be,' said the lawyer. 'Irrespective of that decision, may I offer you my hearty congratulations?'

'You may,' said Bud. 'Now, that other question. That's easy. Just a matter of information. It doesn't look as if we could give our sheriffs any power that is not ours to give. Such, for instance, as the right to make arrests. And it stands to reason that, in case of a sheriff's death or his disability, such power would go back to the hands it came from. That seems simple enough. What I want to know is where a citizen stands about making an arrest in the absence of any officer. If I see a man committing a crime, can I arrest him?'

'That, also, is simple,' said Fletcher. 'In that case, you have the same right to arrest that the sheriff has. But you are not allowed to make a mistake. If you arrest the wrong man, he can make you pay damages.'

'Oh, like that?' Bud considered this information, rolling his eyes thoughtfully from Fletcher to Fowler, and back again; he pushed his fingers through his hair. 'In that case, it's up to me. Bat Cremony can't act as deputy sheriff any more. Somebody shot him today, up on the hill... I did, in fact... Fowler, you're under arrest for conspiracy and arson, and for being accessory to cow-stealing. Anything you say can be used against you. Here are Bat's handcuffs. Slip them on. I'll hold you till further orders... Huh? Bail?... Probably. Bail won't do you any good, Fowler. Nothing will do you any good. You're a gone goose. Hunter came unravelled.'

THE END